"So this was a date?"

"If I'm honest, yes."

Be careful.

The voice rang through her head, but she ignored it. There was nothing careful about being this close, this attracted to the man she was deceiving.

She'd never misled a single person in her life and here she was lying to the one person she actually wanted to get to know on a personal level.

But there was so much chaos going on in her life, how could she even think about something personal with Nigel? He didn't even know her real name.

"I thought you didn't get mixed up with coworkers," she countered.

He slid his fingertip along the slit in her skirt...the one that extended all the way up her thigh. Sophie shivered as her eyes darted from his hand to his face.

"I never have before now."

* * *

From Boardroom to Bedroom
by Jules Bennett is a part of the
Texas Cattleman's Club: Inheritance series.

Dear Reader,

I hope you're all enjoying this installment of the Texas Cattleman's Club series! I'm so excited to bring you Nigel and Sophie's story and all of the juicy scandal that continues.

You don't even know how excited I was to get to write a sexy Brit for this book. Not only do I love a hero with an accent, I also love a determined, headstrong shero. The clash of Sophie and Nigel is instant...in all the good ways.

This was my first time writing a character undercover, and I promise it won't be the last! I loved having Sophie play two roles and try to figure out whether family loyalty or love would win in the end. Poor Nigel has no clue that a spy is in his bed, but he's quite loyal to his own family, so he might not find a way to forgive her.

I can't wait to hear what you all think of Nigel and Sophie! I had such a fun time writing their happily-ever-after!

Happy reading,

Jules

JULES BENNETT

FROM BOARDROOM TO BEDROOM

HARLEQUIN

DESIRE

Special thanks and acknowledgment are given
to Jules Bennett for her contribution to the
Texas Cattleman's Club: Inheritance miniseries.

HARLEQUIN®
DESIRE™

Recycling programs
for this product may
not exist in your area.

ISBN-13: 978-1-335-20889-7

From Boardroom to Bedroom

Copyright © 2020 by Harlequin Books S.A.

This edition published by arrangement with Harlequin Books S.A.

For questions and comments about the quality of this book,
please contact us at CustomerService@Harlequin.com.

Harlequin Enterprises ULC
22 Adelaide St. West, 40th Floor
Toronto, Ontario M5H 4E3, Canada
www.Harlequin.com

Printed in U.S.A.

USA TODAY bestselling author **Jules Bennett** has published over sixty books and never tires of writing happy endings. Writing strong heroines and alpha heroes is Jules's favorite way to spend her workdays. Jules hosts weekly contests on her Facebook fan page and loves chatting with readers on Twitter, Facebook and via email through her website. Stay up-to-date by signing up for her newsletter at julesbennett.com.

Books by Jules Bennett

Harlequin Desire

The Rancher's Heirs

Twin Secrets
Claimed by the Rancher
Taming the Texan
A Texan for Christmas

Texas Cattleman's Club: Houston

Married in Name Only

Two Brothers

Montana Seduction
California Secrets

Texas Cattleman's Club: Inheritance

From Boardroom to Bedroom

Visit her Author Profile page at Harlequin.com, or julesbennett.com, for more titles.

You can also find Jules Bennett on Facebook, along with other Harlequin Desire authors, at Facebook.com/harlequindesireauthors!

For all of the unpublished authors out there...you can do it! Never give up doing what you love.

Prologue

"And the estate, businesses, and all holdings will go to Miranda Dupree."

"You've got to be kidding me." Sophie Blackwood refused to stay silent. She didn't know exactly what to do, what to say, but she couldn't just sit there and do nothing.

How in the hell did her father's ex-wife—his very young ex-wife—manage to sweep the entire inheritance? She was nothing but a gold-digging socialite.

Unacceptable.

Sophie and her father had never been close, but to will everything to the much younger woman who was no longer even his wife was a slap in the face.

Buckley "Buck" Blackwood continued to disappoint her even in death. Sophie glanced over to the woman in question who actually had the nerve to look surprised. Please, like she hadn't dug her claws so deep into Sophie's father... She knew this moment was coming.

Sophie shifted her focus to her brothers who were equally as stunned at the will that their father's lawyer, Kace LeBlanc, kept right on reading from, listing off each item, as if giving everything to an ex were perfectly normal.

Well, Sophie didn't have to stay and listen to this nonsense. She loved her brothers, but there was no love between her and Miranda.

Sophie was surprised her narcissistic step-monster didn't have a whole camera crew here to document this portion of her life. Being one of the star of *Secret Lives of NYC Ex-Wives*—New York's version of *The Real Housewives*—seemed to rule Miranda's life. The woman always had a crew following her, documenting every aspect of her glittery, flashy lifestyle.

This whole scenario really grated on Sophie's last nerve.

Miranda already had millions. She didn't need all of this other stuff from Buck—not the money and not the ranch. Granted, Sophie didn't need it, either, but damn it, she and her brothers were blood relations. Weren't they entitled to something?

Did nobody see the vindictive woman Miranda truly was? There had to be a way to prove she wasn't all high and mighty like so many believed. Sure, the reality show portrayed her as a nurturing, loving woman… Sophie didn't believe that front for a minute.

Channeling the growing pit of anger in her gut, she met Kellan and Vaughn's furious stares as she exited the study of her father's estate.

The only people she cared about were her brothers. They were a team, they always had been. And she knew they would work together to get this travesty of a will overturned. But right now, she was too furious to think, or to concentrate on what their next steps should be. She just needed to get away from her father's house, where she'd never been happy and where she'd just had to sit through a new betrayal. Most people would have been remorseful after a parent's passing, and part of Sophie was sad. Buck was her father, but he'd always been a hard bastard to love. Turns out, that hadn't ended with his death.

As Sophie made her way out into the bright, sunny day, she slid her sunglasses off her head and onto her face. She needed a break. She just wanted an escape even if for just a few days. Royal, Texas, was such a beautiful town and Sophie absolutely loved it here. But like every small town, it was a hotbed of gossip, and this latest bombshell her father had dropped on them was bound to be the talk of the town for weeks. Everywhere she went, people would be whispering, speculating. The thought made her skin crawl.

But gossip can work both ways, she realized after a moment's reflection. If she played her cards right, maybe she could turn the situation to her advantage. All the talking everyone would be doing about the scandalous Blackwood inheritance would lead to lots of talk about Miranda, too. If Sophie could uncover anything—a scandal, or a secret, or maybe whatever bit of leverage Miranda must have held over Buck to get him to disinherit his own children—maybe she could use it to get the will overturned.

Sophie pulled out her cell as she settled behind the wheel of her sporty car. Time to get started.

One

Sophie barely recognized herself in the reflection of the mirrored elevator doors. Flying across the country, getting a complete makeover, and coming up with a whole new identity had been quite the feat.

But persistence paid off...or at least she hoped it would.

She'd traveled to New York to spy on Miranda. She had tried chasing down every possible lead in Royal...but none of them had panned out. After two months of failed attempts, she'd realized she needed to widen her net. If she was going to find anything, it would have to be in New York—and it would have to be in a different persona. No one was willing to spill secrets to the stepdaughter who was known to hate Miranda—but perhaps a new identity would let her slip in under the radar. Sophie had no other idea how to find dirt on her stepmother, so she'd taken a very hands-on approach.

For a week now, Sophie had taken on this new look and role, but she still hadn't gotten used to being someone else. She'd never been this deceitful or this scheming before.

But desperate times and all that.

As the elevator continued to climb toward the floors that housed Green Room Media, Inc. building, she wondered exactly what she'd be doing. She knew she'd landed the job as a temporary consultant, so she hoped this was a position that would get her close to some cutting room floor footage. Maybe she'd even come in close contact with some of the camera crew from *Secret Lives*.

She needed to find some juicy tidbit on Miranda. Something to hold over her or, better yet, to expose her for the gold-digging, conniving attention seeker Sophie believed she was. Something that would let Sophie challenge the will and put Blackwood property back in Blackwood hands, where it belonged. A woman who always flaunted her life and her material possessions all over television didn't need anything more.

Sophie and her brothers deserved their due inheritance. She didn't want to be a whiny child about it, but she'd grown up in Blackwood Hollow and the home held so many memories...memories that shouldn't have been just handed over to Miranda Dupree. Memories she and her brothers made with their wonderful late mother that Sophie wanted to carry over into her own family or her brothers' families one day. That legacy belonged to the Blackwood children, not a second wife. Sophie wanted to do this for her brothers; she wanted them to have what they deserved. They all had plenty of money... This wasn't about that. This was about family, which they'd never considered Miranda part of.

Sophie didn't believe Miranda's sweet and innocent public persona...not one bit. The woman wouldn't be on one of the most scandalous reality shows on television if she were that perfect. There had to be something. Unfortunately, Sophie had made a point of avoiding Miranda as much as possible during her father's short-lived second marriage. She just plain didn't know the woman well enough to know which closets to search for Miranda's carefully hidden skeletons. But surely they were around here somewhere, in the offices of the show that had been the centerpiece of Miranda's life for the past few years.

Secret Lives was a popular reality show based on divorced women living in Manhattan. Of course, ratings hinged on how many scandals the ladies could cause while displaying their lavish lifestyles. It was tacky and tasteless—but it was popular, and it came with a big staff of people behind it, all working to keep it going. That was where Sophie had found her "in."

Sophie had applied for a personal consultant position within the company that produced *Secret Lives*. The security in the place was top-notch, so she'd had to get creative on getting in. No way would a Blackwood be allowed in this office. Not with the death of Miranda's husband so recent. Just the word *Blackwood* would raise too many red flags and Sophie would be shut out before she could even get started.

A temporary job was the perfect opportunity to get inside.

The only glitch? Sophie's popularity from her interior design YouTube channel, *Dream It, Live It*, forced her to alter her look. Usually, popularity was a great problem to have—but for the time being, it was getting in her way. If she didn't have so many loyal followers, she wouldn't have had to go to such great lengths to disguise herself.

Nothing a little hair color, some carefully applied makeup, a sexy pair of cat-eye glasses, a polished jacket and skinny jeans couldn't fix. She typically wore fun dresses because she always found a dress to be much more comfortable than pants. So this outfit was definitely outside of her norm. So was the makeup. She much preferred a natural look, so the red lips were completely out of her comfort zone.

And the hair? She was kind of digging this style. A little fringe around her face and the bold shade of ashy blond made her feel a little sassy. The self-esteem boost was much needed because her nerves were all over the place.

She was hopeful and quite certain nobody would recognize her now.

So here she was, day one of her new job and fully embracing her new identity. Maybe blondes would have more fun.

Oh, and of course her name was the biggest adjustment. That was something she had to fully embrace and always be aware of because if someone tried to get her attention and she wasn't focused enough to recognize her faked name, her cover would be blown.

The elevator stopped and Sophie pulled in a deep breath.

No. She had to stop thinking of herself as Sophie. In this building, and for the next week, she would have to think of herself as Roslyn Andrews. She could remember that, right? A nice combo of Sophie's middle name and her grandmother's maiden name. No problem. At least she'd chosen something somewhat familiar. And she wouldn't have to get used to it for long.

She'd given herself a week timeline to get in,

find the scoop and get out. She didn't like being sneaky—that was quite the opposite of her personality—but she also felt that she and her siblings had been wronged. So, one week. Surely she could do some quick snooping?

The elevator doors slid open and the posh offices of Green Room Media greeted her. The elegant white decor and semicircular desk in the middle of the spacious floor plan were simple, yet classy. The receptionist glanced up from his computer and smiled. She'd talked with him before when she'd come for her interview just days ago. They clearly needed someone fast because they'd hired Sophie on the spot.

"Ah, Miss Andrews. Welcome back. Are you ready for your first day?"

More than he knew. Would it be too obvious if she asked to view cut footage right off the bat?

"Let's do it," Sophie said with a smile. "Just tell me where I'll be."

Craig, she believed his name was, came to his feet and gestured toward the long hallway. "You will actually be working right alongside Mr. Townshend, you lucky girl. He's amazing, but he demands loyalty and precision. His personal assistant is out on maternity leave, but that's no problem. If you need anything, you can always come find me."

Working with Mr. Townshend? As in *Nigel* Townshend? She would be his temporary personal consultant? Sophie didn't know if she was thrilled or terrified to be put in the most inner circle of the entire company…and with the sexiest mogul to ever grace the covers of magazines. He was known as the British Billionaire Bad Boy. Any woman with breath in her lungs knew who Nigel was.

Sophie's heart fluttered and her stomach got a little schoolgirl giddy. Nigel was one very dominating, very powerful man. When Sophie had interviewed, she'd thought for sure she was just going to be a gopher or someone to answer phones. She'd hoped for more, but she also had to be realistic. She'd only been trying to get her foot in the door.

Well, she was in all right. Now she only had moments to mentally prepare to not only meet the sexy Brit but also to compose herself so she didn't come across as some nitwit who didn't deserve this position. She couldn't afford to be let go before she got what she came for.

Sophie hurried to catch up with Craig as he made his way down the wide corridor.

"Are you sure this is the position I'm here for?" she questioned.

Craig came to a halt so fast Sophie jerked to a stop to prevent running into him. He glanced around before leaning in and whispering.

"You didn't hear this from me," he started. "But *Secret Lives* has dipped a little in the ratings and Nigel is taking it upon himself to find out exactly why. He needs fresh eyes to help him fix the situation. That's where you come in."

Well, that was no pressure at all. Nothing like being thrust right into the thick of things on day one. But at least it was a problem that didn't make her feel out of her depth. She did know a little about ratings; after all, she'd built her channel into something of a phenomenon. Maybe she could actually make a difference here, too, *and* get the scoop she needed. A win-win.

"Does he not have anyone who has tried to help so far?" Sophie asked, still positive this position was a mistake.

"His assistant would probably have been a good asset, but she's unavailable and Nigel wants someone from the outside." Craig lowered his voice even more. "I think the show is in jeopardy. He didn't tell me that directly, but… Well, I have some sources."

Oh, she had no doubt the receptionist knew all the ins and outs and was one of the best sources of gossip. Perhaps starting with a little break room talk over lunch would be a good starting point for her own project.

Things were already starting off better than she'd hoped. Surely if Sophie was dealing with the head honcho himself, she could gain access to all the cut footage. But she still had to be careful and calculated about this. There was no room for errors and no way could she raise suspicions. Above all, she couldn't run into Miranda. Even with the blond hair, glasses and completely different wardrobe, Sophie knew her step-monster would recognize her.

"Mr. Townshend is waiting," Craig said as he turned and put his hands on the gold handles of a set of white double doors. "Welcome to Green Room Media."

The doors swung wide and Sophie/Roslyn pulled in a deep breath.

Showtime.

When he'd asked for help, he hadn't expected a lush supermodel turned librarian. The sight of the curvaceous blonde with sultry glasses and a confident smile hit him right in the gut. He was also a fan of glossy red lips.

Those jeans should have been illegal, but he certainly wasn't complaining.

Bloody hell. He didn't have time for this distraction. He hadn't even had time to interview anyone for himself and had trusted his most loyal, dependable employees to do that. But he'd only asked for someone well qualified, professional and polished.

He'd certainly gotten that last part; he had to assume the rest of her credentials were just as impressive as the outward package.

Might as well embrace his new temporary consultant. *Temporary* being the key word. *Off-limits* was also another key word because he never ever fraternized with employees. He liked to date, but he'd never gotten too serious…much to his family's dismay and disappointment.

Most times the Townshends didn't understand why Nigel was in New York, growing his empire, and not back in England, settling down and working on new heirs. He loved his family, he truly valued them and missed them like crazy. But he wanted to branch off from the dynasty and create his own legacy. This company and his shows were bigger than anything he'd ever dreamed. He just needed to continue that trend of growth and success in order to show his family that his goals and dreams truly were worthwhile.

Pushing the family issues aside, Nigel kept his eyes locked on the striking woman in his office. Talk about a test in willpower. If she was going to be working alongside him for weeks or months to come, he would have to remember this was a professional environment. He demanded as much from each of his employees and he would never let them think that he was incapable of meeting those standards himself.

Nigel came to his feet and rounded his desk. He was the boss, time for him to act like one and put these adolescent hormones to rest. His family considered him the infamous black sheep for breaking away, and he was doing his best not to live down to that reputation. Just because a man didn't want to get married and produce a litter of children did not make him a failure.

Of course, his sister was getting married next week and he was a groomsman, so that certainly didn't help matters.

All the more motivation to turn these dwindling numbers around and get *Secret Lives* back on top of the rankings. Maybe then his family would be proud of the work he did.

"You must be Roslyn Andrews," he greeted, turning all of his attention to the new employee. "I'm Nigel Townshend."

Her smile widened as she crossed his office and extended her hand. "It's a pleasure, Mr. Townshend."

"Mr. Townshend is my father," he corrected. "You will call me Nigel."

With a delicate nod, she replied, "Alright, Nigel."

His name sliding through her lips was just as magical and potent as he'd expected. And all of his employees called him Mr. Townshend. He couldn't quite justify the reasoning behind his quick response to her calling him *Mr.* but here they were.

"I had no idea I would be working with you directly," she added. "Can I be honest?"

The combination of that sultry voice and the confident firm grip of her handshake assaulted every nerve ending he had. Her dark eyes flared when he slid his hand into hers.

Well, wasn't this interesting?

She snatched her hand back and adjusted the purse strap on her shoulder. He had to give her credit, though, her smile never faltered.

Self-assurance was a sexy trait. Add that to the alluring outward package and he might be in trouble with this one. Hell, he was already in trouble since they were on a first-name basis after a one-minute meet. He had employees who had worked for him for over a decade who still didn't call him Nigel.

"Please," he replied. "Honesty is our key policy."

She adjusted her tortoiseshell glasses. "I'm even more nervous now that I know I'm working directly with the boss. But, I promise not to let my nerves get in the way of doing my best work."

"I hope you've saved your best work for me because I need the best."

"No pressure," she joked. "I hope I live up to your standards."

"I have no doubt you'll do just fine. I've seen your résumé. The fact that you work in interior design actually appealed to me because I believe designers look at every detail in all aspects of life and that's exactly what I need. And, I'm not sure if you've heard anything, but I'm not difficult to get along with, though I've been told I have a dry sense of humor."

"I have two older brothers. I'm pretty good with holding my own, no matter the jokes."

With her honesty and sense of humor, Nigel could see they'd get along just fine…so long as he kept reminding himself this arrangement was professional and temporary.

How many times could he use those two words?

Probably not enough, because he had a feeling he needed to keep those in the forefront of his mind as long as Ms. Andrews worked by his side.

"Have a seat," he told her, gesturing to the leather chair opposite his desk. "Since I didn't sit in on the interview process, I'd like to get to know a little about you before we begin our day. Like I said, I've seen your résumé, quite impressive, and I've heard my crew speak your praises."

"I'm flattered."

She should be. They'd interviewed a slew of people for this position, but Nigel had put out very specific requirements. Interesting that the most striking, intriguing woman he'd ever met was the one who had landed in his office.

He worked with beautiful women every day. The entire cast of *Secret Lives* consisted of stunning ladies. But something about Roslyn seemed almost wholesome…which was quite refreshing in this field.

Nigel unbuttoned his cuffs and rolled up the sleeves of his dress shirt as he went back to his desk chair. Distance from her would help him keep his head in the game, so would focusing on the sole reason for her employment. He needed a new vision for the show and the only way he could see that happening was to bring in an outsider.

There was no room for attractions or office escapades. The last thing he needed was a sexual harassment lawsuit. Of course, bad press would drive up ratings, but he wasn't about to embarrass his family, put his own reputation on the line or degrade any woman.

He respected women and his new consultant would be no different. There's no reason he couldn't find her attractive and keep a level head about himself…right?

"I saw you recently moved to New York," he began, leaning back in his seat.

Roslyn nodded. "About a month ago. It was time for a change."

"You came from Texas?"

"I did. My family owns a ranch." She eased her purse onto her lap and crossed her legs. "My brothers still live there."

"So why the drastic change?" he asked.

A sadness swept over her face for a second before she tipped her chin and silently gathered herself together. "My father recently passed and it made me realize how fragile life is. I'd always wondered what city life was like and I decided to take the risk."

Taking risks was certainly something he could understand and appreciate. He hadn't gotten this far without stepping outside the proverbial box and taking his own chances in business. He understood her need to be out on her own, away from her family, and he instantly admired her drive and independence.

"I'm sorry for your loss," he told her. "I have to admit, I'm impressed that you took such a leap."

"No time like the present," she stated with that same confident smile that punched him with another dose of arousal.

"You have a degree in design." Nigel glanced at the portfolio photos on his computer screen he'd been looking at before she'd arrived. "These are pretty impressive. Why the switch to media? Did you just want to make a change?"

She shrugged one delicate shoulder. "Why can't I do both? I've always loved design and I'm fascinated by media. Who knows? Maybe one day I can design living spaces and work areas for the stars. This is a good step in that direction."

Nigel leaned forward, lacing his fingers together on his desk. "Is that what you're hoping to gain here? The chance to meet celebrities and get your foot in the door?"

Roslyn opened her mouth, but he quickly held up his hand. "I'm not judging," he added. "I think it's brilliant."

"You got me," she laughed. "I'm always thinking ahead. I figure if I'm going to take the leap into a new kind of market, why not make it a big one? I want to cover a wide variety and when I have my own company, I'll be well versed in all the things."

"That's exactly the type of asset I want on my team," he told her. "What's your favorite food?"

Roslyn blinked, then laughed. "Excuse me?"

"Favorite food."

"Um… I don't know. I guess sushi. Why?"

"I like to have dinner meetings and I want to make sure I choose something you'll enjoy."

He hated most kinds of sushi, but this was New York. Plenty of places served a wide variety that could accommodate both of them. For now, though, he wasn't quite ready to end this talk and he wasn't ready to dive right into work, though that's exactly what he should have been doing.

"Why don't I show you around," he said, coming to his feet.

Craig would've normally tour new employees, but Nigel had already blocked this morning off because he wanted to do so personally… Now he wished he had let Craig retain that honor.

"There are aspects of this company that you should know from day one," he continued. "I want you to be comfortable and think of this as your second home for as long as you're employed here. We're all friendly and, for the most part, we all get along."

Roslyn stood and eased her purse back onto her

shoulder. "That's impressive with such a big corporation. I'm excited to be part of something so positive."

As committed as he was to making sure his staff all worked well together, he wouldn't settle for anything less, Nigel needed a little more drama and action on the set of *Secret Lives*. The show couldn't afford to be all sweetness and niceness all the time. There needed to be a reason for viewers to tune back in, excited to see what would happen next— but right now, he just didn't have the answers.

He did, however, have a new consultant eager to see the offices and he might just have to take her to the penthouse suite and show her that breathtaking rooftop view. The penthouse was used on occasion for special events with the staff since it had a large boardroom table and full kitchen. But, it also had a private en suite that he would sometimes stay in when his office hours became too long and he just needed to crash.

His job right now was to save his show, and this woman may be one of the most striking and gorgeous consultants he'd ever seen, but he needed her and he wasn't going to do anything to jeopardize his show…especially by hitting on his newest hire.

"We'll start with the best part of the entire building."

Nigel gestured to the lift in the corner.

"Your own private elevator?" she asked, with a half grin. "I'm impressed."

"There are perks to being the CEO."

And as the CEO, it was his responsibility to remain 100 percent professional, 100 percent of the time.

He worked with gorgeous women every single day. This shouldn't have been any different...yet it was.

Two

Sophie wasn't sure how to deal with her spiral of emotions as she stood next to Nigel in the elevator. She wished she'd known that she'd be working directly with him. She wished she'd known just how potent this powerhouse truly was. And she sure as hell wished she'd known just how her entire body would heat because this was a completely new territory for her.

Granted she didn't believe anything could've fully prepared her for that heavy-lidded stare, the strong jawline, the right amount of expensive cologne and that polished British accent.

Mercy's sake. She certainly hadn't counted on

how sexy a conversation with a Brit would be. How did any woman in this office get work done? How was *she* going to get work done? She couldn't afford to get fired from her faux job because she was too busy fantasizing about the boss.

The man opened his mouth and a slew of inappropriate thoughts filled her head. But that wasn't why she was here. Though the eye candy certainly didn't hurt.

A man like Nigel Townshend wasn't just a panty-dropper, he was a billionaire bad boy with a bit of a reputation. He always had the sexiest women on his arm at award shows and debuts. He'd been known to date some of the hottest supermodels in the industry, but, to her knowledge, he'd never been seen with the same woman twice, which led her to believe he was a player.

And she was the total opposite, considering she'd never been with a man.

What would it be like to be with a bad boy? Maybe that was precisely what she needed. Perhaps she should give herself to a man who knew exactly what he was doing.

Then again, she wasn't about to announce to a man she just met that she was a virgin. She wasn't ashamed of the fact, and she certainly wasn't sorry she'd spent her years building her career and devoting every waking minute to growing herself as a successful businesswoman and YouTube sensation.

There was no rule or timeline for sex, and she'd do it when she was damn well ready or when a man intrigued her enough to make her want to.

Unfortunately, her new boss intrigued her way more than he should. She could easily imagine him doing a clean sweep of papers off his desk and ripping her clothes off in a heated moment of passion. The clothes would be utterly ruined, of course, but she wouldn't mind sacrificing these skinny jeans.

Why were they called skinny jeans anyway when she clearly had curves and wore a size sixteen? If they were supposed to make her feel skinny, then they were failing.

Regardless, she'd much rather think of Nigel finding her irresistible. Maybe late nights would turn into lingering glances or sensual touching. Not that she thought he'd do anything inappropriate... but a girl could fantasize, couldn't she?

The elevator chimed as the doors slid open. Just in time to pull her from yet another delicious daydream about her new boss.

Good grief. She had enough issues right now. She needed to focus on the job her brothers had trusted her to get done. Getting down and dirty with the CEO of Green Room Media was not quite the angle she'd been thinking of. Besides, she'd promised herself to be back in a week and getting tangled in anything other than her plan would eat up time she didn't have to spare.

Nigel gestured for her to exit the elevator, and as soon as Sophie stepped out, her breath caught in her throat.

"I had the same reaction when I first saw the view," he told her, staying right by her side. "I admit, it never gets old. There's something so timeless, so classy and sexy about the New York City skyline."

From this rooftop penthouse with a wall of glass windows all around the perimeter, Sophie felt as if she could reach out and touch the sun. She had to agree, there was something sexy about this view. Something almost...powerful, like because you were on top of the world that meant the whole world was yours to command.

Even with the wintery conditions outside, she was surprised by how bright the sky seemed to be from this angle.

Wanting to explore each part of this magnificent space, Sophie took one slow step after another as her eyes raked over the rich masculine leather furniture, the chrome fixtures, the simplicity of the lighting and the breathtaking sights of the city. This was definitely a man's space.

She told a slight lie when she'd said she was a wannabe city girl. She mostly stayed to the country life, a laidback style that fit with her personality and the way she designed. City life always seemed so noisy and rushed...not just the cars but everything and everyone else, too. She felt that people were too busy doing their own thing to truly listen to others.

Sophie enjoyed people, she loved chatting and getting to know more about them. How else was she supposed to grow and develop her brand? She had to purposely put herself out there, so over the years, she'd just defaulted to a social butterfly.

Hey, that bold move had paid off, hadn't it? Her YouTube channel ranked in the top ten interior designers of the entire site and she could easily see herself climbing even higher.

"Come closer," Nigel urged, cupping her elbow and escorting her to the windows. "This is the place I escape to when everything downstairs becomes too much."

Sophie glanced from the city below to the man at her side. "And here I assumed there wasn't a thing you couldn't handle."

Nigel's lips quirked. "Don't give away my secret."

"Anything you say is safe with me," she promised. "I'm not here to judge. I'm here to help."

She wasn't here to expose him for anything… unless he was involved in some scandal alongside Miranda. And even then, she didn't want to hurt anyone so she wouldn't do any harm to Nigel.

But Sophie couldn't start digging just yet. She had to ease her way in. Day two, she'd put more of a push on the plot since time was of the essence.

"I imagine there's quite a bit to escape from and many reasons to clear your head." She focused her attention back to the view. "Even the strongest people need to take a mental health break."

"The business can be cutthroat at times," he admitted.

"Too many divas to work with?" she joked, hoping he'd follow her lead.

"The ladies on the show?" he asked, raising his brows. "They're not terrible. A few can be demanding, but overall, they don't cause me too much trouble."

Not what she wanted to hear, but she'd barely gotten started.

Passing the time with Nigel certainly didn't make her angry.

"So, do you live up here?"

Nigel turned his attention toward her. "Oh, no. I've stayed here occasionally after long days of work, but I generally use this to take a break. We've had a few in-house gatherings and private showings up here for the show."

"I don't want to give the wrong impression," she began, hoping she sounded stronger than she felt. "I mean, you know you're an attractive man—"

"*People Magazine* thinks so."

Sophie couldn't help but laugh. "As I was saying, I'm not here for anything other than a great opportunity to learn and be an asset to your team and maybe grow my own skills on the side."

Nigel lifted one dark thick brow.

"Professional skills," she corrected, still unable to stop smiling. Oh, he was a naughty guy, and she couldn't help but like that quality.

"Believe it or not, I need a personal consultant and I take this company very seriously."

He shoved his hands in his pockets and cocked his head in that sexy, arrogant way. There was no doubt Nigel was a force to be reckoned with. He was known around the world, not just for his charm and good looks, but for the way he'd started a company and grown this reality show with high-class divorcees and launched these ladies to superstardom… including Miranda.

"But since we're being honest," he went on. "You obviously have to know you turn heads."

While she wasn't vain, she also wasn't one of those women who feigned being ugly or put herself down in the hopes of gaining compliments. She was also well aware that some men found a plussize woman unattractive. Those were the men she didn't have time for in her life.

While it was gratifying to know that he didn't fall into that category, Sophie didn't want to get into this topic with Nigel. She couldn't afford distractions and she certainly couldn't afford a rumor of the new hire trying to get ahead by flirting, or more, with the boss. Rumors would just draw unwanted attention to her. Miranda couldn't know Sophie was anywhere near this office.

"Well, now that all of that is out of the way, is the attraction going to be a problem?" she asked, holding his gaze and forcing herself to face this head on. She'd always believed in honesty.

Well, except for her current situation, where she was lying about her name and why she was there. But some things were simply a necessary evil.

"No problem," he assured her with a crooked grin and that toe-curling accent.

Maybe other people were immune to Nigel and that sultry voice, but she was new here, new to him. She'd have to put up her strongest steel defenses to keep some resolve between them.

"What else should you be showing me?" she asked. "Maybe where my work space is? Or what projects you'd like me to review?"

He stared like he wanted to say something, but she raised her brows, a silent question waiting on him to answer.

"Craig set up an office next to mine," he told her. "If you're going to be working with me, then I need you close by. The space is not overly large, but you do have a window."

"My own office?"

Sophie certainly hadn't expected that. An office

right next to Nigel? This position was better than she'd ever hoped.

Things were lining up almost too well for her. But she had to ignore the pull she felt toward her new boss and concentrate on what she came here to do. She didn't change her life and her looks just to snag a Brit. Getting the scoop on Miranda was priority number one.

"Does my office come with an elevator?"

Nigel's lips twitched once again, and she noticed every time he became amused his blue eyes twinkled. So silly to notice such things, but she couldn't help but study and try to figure out more about him.

"Sure. It's the one you used to get from the lobby to the reception area."

Sophie rolled her eyes. "Not what I meant," she joked.

She turned her attention back to the view. This was certainly a far cry from the Blackwood Ranch and its open skies with fields of green. Still, this was a different kind of beauty with all the steel combined with old structure. Her designer eye took in all the various shapes and colors. The snow seemed beautiful on the buildings and balconies. She wondered what a fresh snow would look like on the busy streets. Probably kids enjoyed playing in it and throwing snowballs.

The wintery white had her thinking about the re-

cent home office she'd decorated in white and soft
blues with various pops of green.

"Do you always study your surroundings?"

Nigel's question pulled her back as he stepped in
beside her. Sophie glanced over her shoulder and
shrugged.

"Occupational hazard. I love designing and cre-
ating, so my mind is always working."

"You're perfect for this position," he stated.

Sophie swelled with pride, but there was a nig-
gle of guilt. She wasn't here because she wanted
to ensure the greater good of *Secret Lives*. No, she
needed to see those precious unedited outtakes with
Miranda. Surely there were some that revealed be-
haviors or hinted at secrets the producers didn't
want the public to see. There had to be something
juicy there.

"With this being your first day, I won't bombard
you too much. But tomorrow, you better be ready to
work." Nigel gestured toward the elevator. "What
do you say we go check out your office and then
I'll have lunch brought in. Sushi?"

Sophie nodded. "Sounds perfect."

Nigel shoved his hands in his pockets and stared
down at the magnificent skyline. He'd been a complete idiot to bring Roslyn up here earlier. He never
fraternized with his staff.

But from the second she'd stepped foot in his office, she'd had a presence about her that had drawn him in. She'd been poised, confident, polished, sophisticated. She'd been witty and that smile had been like a heavy fist to his gut, knocking the air right out of him. She almost seemed too good to be true.

And she had been honest. Brutally so when she'd confronted him about the attraction between them. Part of him was impressed that she'd been so bold, while the other part had secretly wished she would've acted on her baser impulses.

Bloody hell. What had gotten into him? He couldn't act like this, not even in his thoughts. This company was his everything. He'd come to New York wanting to start his own legacy and he had done a damn good job of it. He couldn't just throw that stellar reputation away because he had the equivalent of a teenage crush. He had to regain control of this situation because Roslyn had been here for one day and he was already second-guessing getting involved with an employee.

He had bigger issues to deal with—like the fact *Secret Lives* needed a major bump in the rankings.

The cell in his pocket vibrated. There was never downtime where he was concerned, not in his position overseeing the company and not when working with several socialites.

He glanced to the screen and saw Seraphina's name.

Seraphina Martinez, or Fee to close friends, was

one of the ladies on *Secret Lives*. She had a big lavish lifestyle and a giving heart. There was nothing low-key about her and she was a fan favorite. Especially after she came out with her bestselling cookbook, *Not Your Mama's Cookbook*.

Nigel turned from the skyline view as he answered the call.

"Fee," he greeted. "How are you?"

"I'm good, thank you. Listen, I just wanted you to know I've been thinking of your offer and I'm not sure I can accept."

Not what he wanted to hear. Seraphina had fallen in love with real-life cowboy Clint Rockwell and they were planning their future together…in Texas. When she's talked about leaving the show, Nigel had tried to entice her into staying in NYC by offering her an impressive package that came with marketing for her cookbook, more airtime and a nice sum of money.

"Now don't turn me down yet, luv," he told her. "We can make this work. I was hoping you'd consider a spin-off."

"A spin-off?" she asked. "Nigel—"

"Just think about it," he interrupted. "A Southern series showcasing you and Clint in this new chapter of your lives would be something the viewers would love."

Not to mention maybe that would be the angle he needed to save his show.

Nigel rubbed his forehead and pulled in a deep breath. He hadn't come this far in his career to allow setbacks to deter him. There was no room to be a failure or even to be mediocre. Staying in the middle of the road in prime-time television might as well be the kiss of death. Another show would come along and bump them right off.

Maybe exploring new territory was something they needed to try. The cast had gone to Texas to Miranda's ranch for the Christmas episodes that had actually caused a slight uptick on the rating's scale.

"Clint is everything to me," Fee went on. "We're a team now, but I'll discuss this with him. I'm not sure he wants all the cameras following us around Texas."

"Just talk to him," Nigel repeated. "I bet an episode centered around your wedding would be a killer series opener."

Silence greeted him on the other end and he knew Seraphina well enough to know she was considering this option. His mind rolled from one idea to the next. This could be the key to those ratings he desperately needed to boost.

"I'm just not sure," she finally stated. "Clint and I really want out of the limelight. We want to start fresh. Those fires that ripped through Royal really put things into perspective for me."

The fires she referred to had ultimately brought her and Clint closer together, but only after putting them both in a lot of danger. The town really pulled through and continued to rebuild. They'd all been affected in one way or another.

"Think about it," he told her. "Talk to Clint."

"I will," she replied. "I know I still have some time left on my contract—"

"We'll deal with that later. See what Clint says first and get back to me. Let's not borrow worries just yet."

"Thanks, Nigel."

He disconnected the call and blew out a sigh. His mind circled back to his new consultant and he wondered if she would be able to offer insight to a new project should Fee agree to it. He didn't want to disclose this new information just yet…but he hoped he could talk Fee and Clint into a spin-off, that may be the answer to his problems.

Also, he wasn't about to spout highly sensitive inside business secrets to a brand-new hire. He missed his assistant right now. Merryl always knew what to do or the right things to say, but she was out with her new baby.

But even if the spin-off happened, and became a real success, Nigel wasn't ready to give up on saving *Secret Lives*. It was the main show he'd started all on his own once he rose to CEO at Green Media Room. He'd come to New York to do something grand, not having anything to do with the Townshend name. *Secret Lives* was what he had to show for all those years of hard work. It was his baby and he would do everything to see it thrive.

With as sharp and witty as Roslyn was, and with her impressive résumé on design, he knew she had a brilliant mind. He planned on putting that to use and making sure his show remained on the air.

Could she be the miracle he'd been waiting on? Was she even capable of doing what he'd been unable to do himself?

He didn't have all the answers, but he knew one thing for certain… He was going to get more time with Roslyn and he couldn't wait.

Three

Sophie had been surprised when she'd gotten to her office the next morning and there had been no sign of Nigel. Craig had said something about an emergency and had given Sophie a list of things to read up on for now. Later, she was to sit in on a meeting with a few of the crew members from the show.

Perfect. A meeting was just the type of jumpstart she needed. No doubt the team would discuss the cast members and Sophie intended to take detailed mental notes on Miranda.

A couple hours later, there was still no sign of Nigel, and Sophie had to admit, she'd found herself thinking about him while she'd been reading the materials in preparation for the meeting.

The only way she could let Nigel in her mind, in her life, would be as a stepping stone to carry out her plan.

Unfortunately, she hadn't expected these new-found responses. No man had ever heated her the way Nigel did. She'd never found herself wanting to throw away her innocence so fast, but Nigel pulled out a whole host of sensations she'd never known existed within her.

Maybe it was the bad boy power trip, or maybe it was the way he'd looked at her like he was imagining her naked. Maybe it was the way he could banter with her like they'd known each other for years.

Regardless, she'd never had an intimate relationship, let alone a fling. That was the main reason she'd had to be completely honest yesterday. She didn't want Nigel to believe she was here for him or give him the wrong impression of her true nature.

Well, her sexual true nature.

If she'd met him under different circumstances—where she wasn't lying to him, where she'd have had the time to actually get to know him—she might see where this attraction would lead.

But the fantasy was moot and she had to remain focused.

Sophie grabbed the documents and her cell off her desk and stepped from her office. The notes on marketing and upcoming filming ideas regarding *Secret Lives* had been interesting from a viewer standpoint…if she bothered tuning into the popular reality show. And she actually might religiously watch the show if Miranda weren't on there. The other ladies were in fact really interesting.

Sophie had watched a couple of times, but just the sight of Miranda acting all sweet and kissing cheeks with her bling sparkling in the lights was enough to make Sophie gag and change the channel.

The meeting room was down two floors and Sophie made her way into the elevator with a few other employees she didn't know. They chattered about office gossip, none of which was useful to her.

When Sophie stepped into the meeting room, she found a seat at the end of the long table and smiled at the young man next to her.

"You're new," he said. "I'm Miles."

Sophie nodded. "Roslyn. Nice to meet you."

"These meetings are so silly," he muttered as he leaned into her. "Any of this information could be sent in an email, but Mr. Townshend is really cracking down. He's actually been on edge more lately. The ratings have dipped lower than ever."

Sophie kept quiet as Nigel entered the boardroom. His baby blues swept over the handful of employees before landing on her. A thrill shot through her and she had no idea how the man exuded such power in a room full of people and with just one simple look.

"I gather you all read the marketing notes," he began as he took a seat at the head of the table. "We're taking a new approach to the social media aspect and I want to make sure we're all on the same page."

Sophie listened intently as they went around discussing the new segments and how to best maximize the social media content. She watched as Nigel seemed to take to heart each employee's suggestions and she had to admire a man who didn't pawn staff meetings off on other employees or use them as a platform to spout his own ideas without listening to anyone else. He didn't patronize any of his crew members or make them feel like their ideas weren't worthy or of value. That spoke volumes for what he was like as a CEO.

Sophie also wanted to chime in along with everyone else and tell them they were going about this completely wrong. From personal experience, she knew what pulled people in and she knew how to dive into a certain market to really target the niche market.

Added to that, consulting was also about listening to all of the facts before offering up her opinion or suggestions. She was new and didn't want to step on toes on her second day, so she chose to just remain silent.

Sophie did take down notes on things she would like to discuss with Nigel in private. She'd recommend different angles on their current marketing plans. After all, she hadn't blown up on YouTube for nothing. She liked to think she'd done a few things right and knew how to grab the public's attention. Of course it didn't hurt she excelled at her career choice, but she'd had to market herself and become a brand to get that initial attention.

Her eyes darted back to Nigel and...

Speaking of attention. He stared at her in a way no man ever had before—like he wanted more than her thoughts. And in a room full of people.

Someone else started speaking, but Sophie didn't hear what they said. Nigel broke the spell by glancing away, but Sophie couldn't quite focus for the rest of the meeting.

Once they concluded, she gathered her things and headed back to her office. That meeting hadn't produced anything she could use to further her plan. In fact, very little was said about the show's stars at all. When filming was mentioned, it was mostly locations being brought up for upcoming shots and how they would be marketing the show by implementing new ideas.

So, since there was nothing she could do right now to dig into Miranda's dirty secrets, she decided to stay in the marketing headspace and pull together some ideas and suggestions for the show.

Sure, she wouldn't be staying long, but it would still look suspicious if she didn't have *any* work to show for her time on the clock. She couldn't just ignore the fact Nigel believed her to be legit. So long as she kept up this charade, she could possibly find everything she needed.

Sophie had a spreadsheet she'd used when first getting started on YouTube—basically the dos and don'ts and what worked and didn't work when it came to brand promotion. The marketing field was like a strategic game and if the players didn't know what move to make next, the entire plan could be for naught.

She realized there was an entire team here, but Nigel had wanted fresh eyes and that's where she came in.

The moment Sophie stepped inside her office and circled her desk, she glanced toward the doorway and let out a yelp.

"I didn't mean to startle you."

Nigel leaned against the doorjamb, his arms crossed over his broad chest. His hair was just a bit mussed, as if he'd raked his hands through it after the meeting.

Clearly she'd been so focused on her own thoughts, she'd missed the fact he'd practically been right behind her when she'd come in.

"No, it's fine," she replied, laying her things down. "I'm actually glad you're here."

"Is that right?"

"I have some things I want to run by you regarding a few marketing suggestions," she replied, ignoring the way he just stood there, staring, like he'd rather be doing anything else than talking about work.

"Why didn't you voice your thoughts during the meeting?" he asked, his brows instantly furrowed.

"Well, my job is to listen to all of the material before tendering my opinion," she informed him. "Plus, it's my second day and I wasn't sure your employees wanted to hear that I think most of their ideas are wrong."

Nigel studied her for a moment before he let out a bark of laughter and dropped his arms. "I do appreciate all of this honesty you provide. But, if we're going to talk, I say we should do so over lunch. Meet me in the penthouse in thirty minutes."

"I need about forty-five," she stated. "Trust me. I've got something to share with you."

He stared at her for another minute. Sophie didn't miss the crackle of tension. Even if she was here as a ruse, she had to be up front because she'd never been good at hiding her feelings. There was only so much lying she could handle.

"Listen," she started. "The attraction here is…"

Nigel quirked a brow. "Yes, it is," he agreed with a smile. "But, I would never get involved with an employee. I'm strict about that. Especially now when my sole focus needs to be on the show."

Sophie nodded. "Okay, good. Because I didn't come here for a fling or anything else. I just can't stand tension and I had to talk about the proverbial elephant."

"I appreciate your bold honesty."

With a shrug, Sophie sighed. "It can put off some people."

"Men?"

She nodded.

"Then they're fools."

There it went again…that crackling tension. She waited on him to say more, but he wouldn't. He'd already made it clear he didn't socialize with employees. Too bad he didn't know she wasn't a legit staff member. Though he probably wouldn't be too thrilled with her if he knew why she was really there. Maybe it was better this way. They couldn't be together, but at least she knew he wanted to be.

"I'll see you upstairs in forty-five minutes," she told him, needing to shut this moment down.

Nigel offered her a grin and nod, then he turned and was gone. Sophie blew out a breath the moment he stepped away from her office. Revisiting the attraction issue wasn't going to get either of them anywhere they needed to be. She had to remain focused and so did he. They both had outside issues that needed their full attention...though he didn't realize that.

And had she seriously considered getting into something—a fling—with her fake boss? Sophie was either sleep deprived or else she had completely lost her self-control when it came to Nigel because she'd gone this whole time without giving herself to a man. Was she really ready to jump into it all because of a sexy accent and some sexy stares?

No, she wouldn't lose sight of why she was here. Her job was to find what she needed to secure her and her brothers' family legacy. Nothing more.

If maintaining her cover meant that her business ideas helped Nigel and she assisted in making any part of his team stronger, that would just be extra.

Sophie figured by the end of this charade everyone would win.

Nigel was still smiling when Roslyn arrived at the penthouse suite. He should've kept this meeting in his office, all professional, but that was not what had come out of his mouth, so here they were.

The woman was quite intriguing. He didn't know her well, but everything he'd uncovered so far seemed so fascinating. The fact she'd basically called his staff incompetent both irked and amused him. He couldn't wait to see what she thought she knew that could beat the carefully crafted plans from the well-educated, experienced team he'd personally vetted for these positions.

Maybe her ideas held merit or maybe she was just full of herself. Either way, he admired her for having the confidence to speak up…as if he needed more reasons to find her attractive.

Today she wore a fitted pair of black ankle pants with a black jacket and red pumps. Those damn pumps matched her lips. She looked like a '50s pinup come to life and, like an idiot, he'd purposely put himself alone with her. But he had a feeling she could have shown up wearing sweats and sneakers and he'd still have found her just as striking because his attraction wasn't just to the exterior… She was damn smart and bold. Qualities he couldn't ignore.

And that was not smart of *him*. Not if he wanted to retain control over his emotions. He had to push aside his desires and the way his body responded when she looked at him. He already had one mess on his hands with the rankings of *Secret Lives*, he didn't need a scandal by having a fling with his consultant.

"I had lunch brought up," he told her as she stepped from the elevator. "There's quite a variety. I assume you don't eat sushi all the time."

"I do like other things, you know." She carried her laptop and cell and walked to the chrome-and-glass desk in the corner to put her things down.

"But I skipped breakfast, so anything sounds great at this point."

While they made their plates, he took note of things she liked, things she overlooked. He found he wanted to know everything about her…and please her with this knowledge in the days to come.

"So, tell me, what do you know that my very well-trained staff doesn't? This is what I needed when I searched for a consultant. I need that fresh look on things from someone who isn't in the industry, but who still pays attention to all details."

They took a seat at the desk across from each other. Instead of starting on her lunch, Roslyn pulled up her computer and swiveled it around to show him a graph she'd created.

"This is fairly rough, but I plugged in a few numbers to give you an example of what I'm about to explain."

Intrigued, he ignored his lunch, as well. He watched as she pointed from one colored area to the next. She'd clearly pulled numbers from the latest rankings that had been just discussed at the meeting. How the hell had she been so fast?

"You can see that the targeted viewers are mainly on social media during these times. But your posts are going up during different times and missing their mark." She noted the difference, then clicked onto another screen and another graph. "The posts are good—but most of them are getting lost in everyone's feeds." She pointed out a few posts that had come the closest to hitting the time slots she'd highlighted. "Look at the difference in engagement—the uptick in likes, retweets, responses. If you put up the juicier posts—the ones with more exciting content—in these time slots, I think you'd see huge results."

Nigel stared at the screen and listened to everything she said. All of her thoughts made perfect sense...which made him wonder why his very well-paid team hadn't considered this strategy before. This was the first he'd seen anything like this.

"You did all of this in the few minutes since we spoke?" he asked, turning his attention back to her.

"Well, I admit I jotted most everything down, but I also made some mental notes, so I may have missed a few of the opinions," she admitted. "But, it was merely a matter of plugging numbers in. I've taken quite a few online marketing classes, so I just used what I've learned. It's a rough draft, like I said, but I can get more concrete examples before the next meeting if you'd like."

Sexy, sophisticated and smart. He was in a hell of a lot of trouble here.

"You've taken marketing classes?" he questioned after a moment.

She nodded and shifted her computer aside, then pulled her plate and bottled water in front of her. "I love design but I knew I wouldn't be able to grow and reach more clients if I didn't understand how the whole social media system works. I needed to know how to interpret all the ins and outs. No matter how good I believe my ideas are for decor, I won't get anywhere without understanding the dynamics of every aspect of business."

The more she talked, the sexier she became. She adjusted her glasses, not in a coy flirty way, but out of necessity as they started to slip. A wayward strand of blond hair landed across her forehead and she swiped it back, tucking her hair behind her ear.

"So basically you want to practice the 20/20/20 method, as well," she went on, oblivious to the fact the more she discussed business, the more turned on he became. "Not only posting during the right times, but also actively engaging with various followers. The rule is twenty new followers, twenty new comments, twenty new likes. Now, with *Secret Lives* being so successful, we can bump that number up. Viewers want to feel important, like they have that personal relationship or connection to the ladies."

She plucked a juicy strawberry from the plate, studied it and popped it in her mouth. Nigel had never been so jealous of a piece of fruit.

"I would recommend the cast of the show following the same method," she added. "They're your ticket to new viewers. If they aren't hyping up the show, nobody else will."

"They post quite a bit during the season," he replied.

"But what do they do in the off seasons? And are they posting the right content?" she countered. "Are they getting viewers intrigued for another episode? Hinting at scandal or something teasing to pull more people into watching the new shows?"

Nigel pulled up various social media accounts from the cast and scrolled through. He quickly saw that she was right—their content needed to be more tailored, more focused. He had his marketing team divided into specialty groups, each one focusing on one specific area. Yet in less than two days, Roslyn had managed to nail down exactly what they needed and even had a damn graph to prove her point.

After several moments of silence, Nigel placed his phone on the desk and pulled his own plate over. He picked at his food, rolling around all the information inside his head.

"If I overstepped—"

"No." He stared across the desk. Roslyn didn't seem insecure as she met his gaze, which just raised his admiration another notch. "You didn't overstep. These are things I need to know and you're going above and beyond in such a short time."

"Good. I didn't want to step on toes, but I was hired for a reason."

His respect for this new hire continued to climb.

Maybe she wasn't too good to be true. Maybe she was just this amazing and he'd hit the jackpot.

With each moment he spent with her, he found her beauty taking a backseat to her brilliant mind. Looks would only get someone so far in life and Roslyn was proving to be a great asset on many levels.

Damn shame he didn't get personal with employees. Since his position was so prestigious and everything he'd wanted when he came to New York, he wouldn't jeopardize that for anything. He wanted his family in England to be proud of what he'd done. He didn't want them to think he just came here and bounced from one beautiful woman to another. Yes, he dated quite a bit, but he also didn't flounce it all over the media, and he never ever dated someone from the show…or his office staff.

Roslyn was exactly the type of woman he hadn't known he was looking for. If she weren't working for him, then he wouldn't have minded getting to know her on a more personal level and building trust. Trust was so hard to come by in this industry when most people were only looking out for themselves and how they could get ahead.

But while a more intimate kind of trust wasn't an option between them, that didn't mean he couldn't enjoy Roslyn's company, perhaps more than he did with any other employee.

"If you start with Seraphina's account, for example." Roslyn pulled up the page and turned her phone toward Nigel. "Even her bio could be catch-ier."

Nigel felt the brewing of a headache and shook his head. "Seraphina may not be part of the show much longer."

He hadn't meant to let that out, but his instinct told him Roslyn could be trusted. She'd gone to great lengths to prove herself and if he wanted someone to help him grow in the rankings, she would need all the pertinent information.

Roslyn's dark eyes widened. "Oh, um… I wasn't aware. Not that you needed to tell me."

"It's okay," he replied. "I actually just found out recently that she was considering leaving—though of course, we don't want her to go. I was on the phone with her this morning offering her another option. That's why I was a few minutes late to the meeting."

"Does she want to leave?" Roslyn asked. "What will she do?"

Nigel had kept asking her that very question. "She's moving to Texas with a cowboy she met while she was filming down there. She and Clint are getting married."

Roslyn smiled. "Well, that's great news for them and for the show. That's a huge marketing tactic and an angle that every viewer would love. A happily-ever-after for one of your favorite ladies is like gold."

"Which is why I want her and Clint to do a spin-off," he confided. "I've talked to her about it, but she's not sure Clint would be on board."

Roslyn's gasped. "Yes. A spin-off would be perfect. There's nothing more valued than a real-life love story and people put so much faith in such fairy tales."

"Fairy tales?" he questioned. "You don't believe in true love?"

Roslyn shrugged. "It's not often I see it in action. I mean, I love my brothers and they love me. Actually, my oldest brother has found love, but that's a rarity, in my opinion. I can't say I had love from my father and he certainly didn't have it for my mother. He cheated on her and made no qualms about it even after she passed away of a stroke. I guess I'm just jaded on the whole thing."

Interesting. For someone so passionate about her work, it seemed that Roslyn went the complete opposite way when it came to her personal life.

"So if a man showered you with bouquets of your favorite flowers, you wouldn't be tempted to fall a little in love?"

Roslyn laughed as she sat her phone down and reached for her bottled water. "A bouquet of flowers is so clichéd. If a man brought me a single stem with heartfelt words, that would mean more than an entire expensive bundle."

"So you need pretty words?" he asked.

"I don't *need* anything," she corrected. "I deserve someone who is honest and wants to open his heart to me alone. I just don't think that man exists."

Nigel processed her words, understanding pain masked by a wall of defense.

"And what about you?" she asked. "Do you believe in true love?"

"I don't think it's some type of unicorn myth, but I haven't exactly had time to devote myself to looking. Though my grandmother is more than ready to marry me off and start another line of Townshends."

"That sounds a bit archaic," she scoffed.

"You don't know my grandmother. The woman is a force to be reckoned with. I'm terrified of her."

Roslyn laughed. "Well, maybe you should be looking for Mrs. Townshend."

Or maybe he should work on figuring out how to get Roslyn out of his every waking fantasy. How could he even think about another woman with the way he wanted her?

And what Nigel wanted, he always got.

Now if he could figure out how the hell to get around his own rule of not getting involved with his employees all while saving his show, he could retain his sanity and stay in control.

Four

Sophie pushed away from her desk and came to her feet, adjusting her shirt over the top of her black pencil pants. She really wished she hadn't gone all out in the transformation. She missed the comfortable yet fashionable dresses that had become her trademark. A good maxi and flip-flops sounded perfect right about now.

But with it being winter in New York, she was happy for the extra layers. Mercy, that wind could be brutal. She certainly missed the warmth and sunshine back in Royal, but she truly felt like she was getting somewhere here…and she didn't mean with just Nigel.

A tap on her door frame had her lifting her head to see Craig. "Hey. Mr. Townshend called and wants you to meet him for dinner. He texted you the address and time, but he wanted me to follow up with you."

Sophie reached for her phone on her desk. "I didn't hear anything come through," she muttered.

She tapped the screen and, sure enough, there was a message from Nigel about dinner, but she'd also missed two from her brothers. Clearly she needed to check in.

"Got it." She smiled at Craig and waved her phone. "I forgot I put it on vibrate earlier."

"No problem," he replied. "So, how's everything going? Settling in okay?"

Sophie nodded. "Seems to be going really well."

"I overheard Mr. Townshend chatting with a few guys from the camera crew." Craig stepped into her office and lowered his voice. "He mentioned you and some of your ideas for capturing snippets for teasers for social media."

Sophie couldn't help but feel a swell of pride. Over their lunch yesterday, she'd not only discussed posts but also various ways to showcase small segments to continue to draw new viewers in. She was trying to appeal to all walks of life, no matter the stage a woman was at. Divorced, married, stay-at-home-mom, career woman, whatever. There was something in each cast member that could appeal to any potential female viewer.

But on the coattails of her pride came the guilt. While she may actually be good at her job, she hated being deceitful. Nigel and Craig and everyone else she'd encountered were so nice to her, making sure she felt like part of the team.

"Well, I just hope those ideas pay off for *Secret Lives*," she replied.

"Seraphina might be off the show." Craig cringed. "That won't be good."

So apparently it was still just at the rumor stage—Nigel must not have told anyone but her. She felt quietly honored at his faith in her discretion. Sophie might want to pull out all the gossip on Miranda she could, but she wasn't about to add anything to the mix or get into the lives of the other women. And there was no way she'd betray anything Nigel trusted her with…unless Miranda's name came into the mix.

"That would be a shame," she replied. "It seems all the women mesh really well together."

Craig shrugged. "I don't know. Between the ratings and the potential loss of one of the cast members, I just hope the whole show doesn't go under. But, that's just my nerves talking. We still have some great women."

"Do you have a favorite?" she prompted.

Craig smiled. "Doesn't everyone? I'm partial to

Miranda. That whole Southern charm she has is so fun. Plus, she's probably the nicest out of the bunch." He grinned at her. "You look surprised—did you get a different impression of her? It's always difficult to tell on screen, but even when the camera is off, she treats the staff with respect and is always so friendly."

Ugh. Not at all what she wanted to hear. But that was just one opinion and Sophie had just gotten started.

"Nobody can be that sweet all the time," she countered with a smile to soften her doubts. "I bet you know some juicy dirt on all the cast."

Craig playfully raised a hand to his lips and mimed turning a lock before he shrugged.

"I knew it," she joked, but she wished he'd give up a little more information. "How long have you been here, Craig?"

"Three years."

"So you've definitely seen the ladies at their best and their worst."

He nodded and leaned his shoulder against the wall. "You could say that. There have been a few cat fights behind the scenes."

"Oh, I'm sure," she added. "Strong, independent women like that? There would have to be some alpha tendencies that clash."

"They do," he agreed. "For the most part, though, they get along. Maybe that's why the ratings have dipped. People expect more drama from such reality shows. These ladies usually pull for each other because they all understand what it's like to be a divorced woman trying to start over."

Or trying to dig her greedy claws into things that don't belong to her.

"Plus, they all really bonded over the fires that broke out while they were helping Miranda deal with her new inheritance after her ex passed away," Craig added. "All of that was something out of a movie."

Yeah, Sophie was well aware of what a nightmare all of that had been…and still was. The inheritance, the fires. Royal was still recovering and the Texas Cattleman's Club clubhouse is undergoing yet another renovation. Only a few years ago the entire place had been revamped and updated. With these recent fires, a portion of the beautiful main building had been damaged.

But Royal was a tight community. There may be drama and gossip, but when push came to shove, everyone pulled together.

Sophie's cell vibrated on her desk and she glanced to the screen.

It was her brother Kellan.

"If you'll excuse me," she told Craig. "I need to take this."

"Of course," he told her, pushing off the wall and

heading to her door. "I'll let Mr. Townshend know you'll meet him later."

She waited until she was alone before she took a seat behind her desk and answered the call.

"Kellan. What's up?"

"Irina and I haven't heard from you for a few days. Any news?"

Irina and Kellan were madly in love after an affair that led to them realizing they were perfect for each other. Irina had been their father's maid, and had a dark past as a mail-order bride, but Kellan treated her like royalty.

"Nothing I can use," Sophie admitted.

The only thing she'd gained was a stack of steamy fantasies about her utterly delicious boss... but Kellan probably didn't want to hear that. Divulging the fact that she was working right alongside the hottest man who gave her all the feels and all the dirty thoughts might not be the best idea. And yet, who could blame her? It wasn't her fault she was having a difficult time focusing whenever Nigel was near.

"Are you doing okay?" he asked. "I worry."

Always the worrier where she was concerned— and even more so now that she was in New York undercover.

"I'm fine and I promise to let you guys know as soon as I see or hear anything useful," she vowed.

"It's just taking more time than I thought. So far, Miranda is dubbed a saint."

Kellan snorted. "Doubtful. Maybe you haven't talked to the right people."

"Well, there are quite a few here," she admitted. "I'm working my way through."

Sophie kept her voice low since her door was open, but she hadn't heard any activity out in the hallway.

"I'm hoping to get into the film room and check out some of the cut scenes," she murmured.

"That might be the ticket, and the proof, we need. If she admits to manipulating Dad, or using some trick to push the will through, we'll be able to challenge it in court," Kellan agreed.

"How's everything in Royal?" she asked.

"Same. Irina is still planning our big belated honeymoon trip and I'm working on another deal with a developer in Houston."

Sophie loved that her brother had found such happiness with Irina. They'd come together after Irina had suffered an abusive marriage. Buck had rescued her by offering her a job and a way out, but Kellan was the one who had truly healed her heart. Kellan and Irina were meant for each other and Sophie was glad they'd finally come back together after years of knowing each other and dancing around the attraction.

The Blackwood children deserved their own

happiness, but Sophie wasn't sure settling down with some perfect guy was in the cards for her. She certainly wasn't looking for love. Such an emotion didn't exist for everyone and she wasn't holding her breath that it would happen to her.

But lust? Yeah, that was not an issue.

Nigel made her want to throw out her vow to hold on to her virginity until the right man came along. She'd decided long ago there wasn't a right man or anyone she felt worthy enough to give that piece of herself to.

She didn't want to have sex just for the sake of having sex. Maybe she was in the minority with that line of thinking, but she didn't answer to anyone and she was proud of the fact she didn't sleep around to feel good about herself.

Nigel, on the other hand, had her envisioning flings and heated nights…and naughty whispers in her ear with that sexy British accent. Maybe if he'd come along sooner in her life, or if she were here under different circumstances, she would see just what could happen if she let herself go and let her desire guide her decision-making.

"Sophie?"

She jerked her attention back to the conversation. "Sorry," she replied. "I got distracted."

"You sure you're okay?" Kellan asked. "You don't have to do this. We can find another way to contest the will and make Miranda give up what's ours."

"I swear, I'm fine," she insisted. "Listen, I need to get back to work, but I'll be in touch."

"Love you."

"I love you, too," she replied before she ended the call.

Sophie glanced at the time and realized she only had a few hours before she had to meet Nigel. There were a couple angles she was working on for him and she wanted to finish up. The more she proved to be useful, perhaps the more he would trust her with the show's secrets. He'd already disclosed Seraphina's personal issue. He was bound to know *something* about Miranda that went beyond public knowledge.

Sophie's entire goal here had hinged on her finding useful gossip or some sort of concrete proof that Miranda had lured Buck into giving his estate to her. Sophie didn't believe her father had done so just because. But even if he had, Sophie didn't think she and her brothers should just be cut out of a family legacy.

Since Sophie was working so closely with Nigel, perhaps she should find ways to use that to her advantage. He would know these women better than probably anyone on the set. They trusted him and confided in him.

Sophie wasn't about to use her body to get information—she would never do something like that. But spending extra time with Nigel over dinners or coming up with new ideas to get into his office for extra minutes could lead to conversations she could use later.

After all... Nigel had clearly made it apparent he was interested. Maybe he would trust her with more and then she could get back to Royal...before she ended up losing her innocence.

Five

Nigel came to his feet when Roslyn entered the private room. He'd requested his usual spot on the second floor of Manhattan's poshest restaurant. He wanted no interruptions.

"I'm so sorry I'm late." Roslyn pulled off her red scarf and coat, then shook out her golden hair. "It takes quite a bit longer to get around the city than where I'm from."

"Country girl," he joked, gesturing for her to take a seat in the curved booth next to him.

The hostess took Roslyn's coat and scarf before leaving them alone.

The flickering candle and the tight bundle of

white roses in a gold vase on the table set a romantic vibe, one he wasn't purposely trying to create. He'd wanted to spend time with her, and he'd wanted a good dinner. Why couldn't he have both? The decor wasn't his fault—it came with the room.

"I'll take your crazy traffic into account next time we meet," she told him.

"I'll send my driver next time," he replied.

"That's not necessary. I doubt you do that for your other employees."

True, but she wasn't just any employee. An argument he wasn't going to have now. He'd just send the car next time and she would have no choice but to allow him to make her life easier.

"Which reminds me of something I've been meaning to ask," she added, turning to face him. "Everyone in the office calls you Mr. Townshend, yet you told me to call you Nigel."

Busted.

"You're working closer with me than most of them do. Would you like a glass of wine?" he asked, instead of going in circles with an argument he'd ultimately win anyway.

"White, please. And nice dodge."

Nigel merely smiled with a wink as he got the waiter's attention and ordered drinks. Once they were alone again, he shifted toward her.

"Craig tells me you've been busy all day. I believe the words he used were *huddled over your computer and muttering to the keyboard.*"

Roslyn smiled and tipped her head. "I may have been working on a few things."

"Such as?"

She turned and reached inside her bag and procured a folder. "I was hoping you'd ask. I went ahead and came up with some possible scenarios for some upcoming segments. Just a few things that would entice viewers to keep tuning in and expand your base."

Intrigued, and more than turned on at her work ethic and passion, Nigel eased closer. He wanted to get a look at what she'd brought, but he'd be lying if he claimed he didn't want to just get closer, to inhale that sexy floral scent that permeated from her. For such a country girl, she seemed to blend right in with this city life. She worked hard, hustled harder and had class, beauty and brains that just begged for anyone around her to notice.

Why was he torturing himself? Why didn't he just find another woman to spend time with…and one that would guarantee a satisfying ending to the evening?

Because none of the women he knew fascinated him like Roslyn Andrews.

Nigel listened to her talk, watched as she flipped from one graph to the next and even discussed pulling in a few celebrity appearances, perhaps at a cocktail party hosted by one of the ladies.

"Because if they hype up the event on their social media, you will instantly expand your viewer base," she finished.

Nigel extended his arm along the back of the booth. "Impressive."

Her smile beamed and her eyes sparkled. "I really think the solution to your problem is simple, but it will require a little grunt work."

Story of his life. He'd never met anyone who worked harder than him…until now. But her ideas and ingenuity were the exact match he needed not only to keep his show afloat but to rise higher than ever in the rankings.

"Let's take a break," he told her. "I skipped lunch and I'm hungry enough to order one of everything."

Roslyn laughed. "I'm not sure I'm that hungry, but I'd love an appetizer or bread to go with this wine."

They ordered and once they were alone again, Nigel wanted to dive into more about her personal life. There was a need to learn everything about her, which he couldn't explain, and wasn't even going to try. It had been a long time since a woman intrigued him like Roslyn. Everyone in the office who had met her so far had been just as fascinated and impressed by her work ethic and her drive… Her sweet

Southern accent also went a long way in charming some of the men.

Nigel didn't like it, but he couldn't blame them. Roslyn was the complete package.

"So, you came to the city because you wanted a change after your father's passing," he began. "Are you enjoying the lifestyle here? Other than the traffic, that is."

"It's definitely an adjustment. I'm not sure I'd ever get used to all the chaos. Texas is a big state and I'm used to land and green grass with sunny blue skies." She hesitated before tipping her head and leveling his gaze. "Where are you from originally?"

She wanted to turn the tables? Fine by him. He didn't mind sharing his backstory, especially if that meant she was just as interested in him as he was in her. Maybe that was his ego talking, but he didn't miss the way she looked at him. He'd been hit on and charmed by many women—a man in his powerful position was prone to such things. Roslyn wasn't trying to seduce him with her pretty words or sexy clothes…yet she did all the same.

Everything about her turned him on and the differences between them kept tugging at him to uncover more. Because the more he found how different they were, the more he realized how much they complimented each other.

"My family is back in Cumbria, England," he

told her. "Beautiful countryside and I love it when I'm there, but I also love the city. No reason I can't have the best of both worlds. I understand the appeal of vast land with green as far as the eye can see. That sounds like where I grew up."

"I bet you have horses," she guessed, curling her fingers around the stem of her wine glass. Yet, she never took her eyes off him as she smiled.

"We do," he replied. "It's something my grandmother and I always shared a passion in. When I go home, we always have a date at the stables."

"You've mentioned your grandmother before. I take it you two are close."

Roslyn shifted in her seat, causing the strands of her hair to brush against his hand behind her back. He couldn't resist sliding the ends between his fingers, his eyes darting to the golden strands.

"Your hair is so damn soft," he muttered before he could stop himself.

"Your grandmother."

"I've never felt her hair."

Roslyn laughed. "We were talking about your grandmother."

"We were, but I'd rather talk about you."

She hesitated for a second and the moment was broken. He pulled his arm back, not wanting to make her uncomfortable or come across as a creepy boss. Hadn't he told her he wouldn't get involved? How did she continue to pull him in? It was that damn mind of hers. She was too fascinating, too intoxicating. He continually wanted more.

"Tell me more about this hometown of yours," he said. "You know, Miranda also lived in Texas for a time."

"I'm aware," she replied. "I made it a point to study up on all the cast. I assumed that was part of my job, right?"

"Always circling back to work." Nigel shook his head and reached for his glass. "I've never met anyone who cares about work as much as I do."

"Well, I care about my job and making a good impression," she stated. "I've always believed anyone can make a difference, no matter how small their position or their financial background."

She had the perfect words for everything. Literally everything.

He'd been toying with an idea since the last staff meeting, but he'd thought it too soon to jump the gun. Now, though, he wasn't so sure. Maybe his idea was exactly what was best not only for him, but for the company.

"I want to run something by you," he told her.

"Okay. Are we back to discussing work?"

Nigel couldn't help but smile. "For the time being. What do you say to working as the lead on the marketing for Serephina's wedding? I mean, not the actual wedding, but the marketing of the buzz around the show? If you could draw something up that I could show her, maybe we could convince her to air their nuptials—possibly into a new spin-off."

The idea rolled out of him as he continued on, hoping she would take this on. Roslyn's eyes widened, her mouth dropped open. After a moment, she regained her composure and took a sip of her wine.

"Well, I'm flattered you'd consider me for one of the most important episodes if that happens." She muttered the word as if rolling the idea around in her mind, thinking out loud so as to clarify her answer in some way. "I would love to draw something up for you. I hope that will convince Serephina to agree to the show."

A heavy weight lifted from his shoulders. Things seemed to be falling into place and Nigel was certain that everything he ever wanted was right in front of him.

"Who knows what will happen, but I'm confident with your plans and ideas. Fee will have a difficult time turning this down. She loves the other ladies and this show, and she still wants to see everyone succeed. I have faith in you that you're my key to getting this show back at the top of the rankings."

Something passed over her face, something he couldn't quite identify. After a moment, Roslyn squared her shoulders and gave a clipped nod.

"I won't let you down."

* * *

Sophie drained her second glass of wine and wondered yet again what the hell she'd gotten herself into. Agreeing to another project for Nigel? She didn't have time for all of this. She needed to get in and out of this job and this persona before Miranda knew she was here. She needed to get back to her life in Royal and back to her legacy.

But she couldn't turn Nigel down. When he looked at her with that hope in his eyes, she knew how much he wanted this show to thrive. She saw how hard he worked, how invested he was in the program he'd created. Isn't that what she wanted? She wanted the life she worked so hard for, the life she was entitled to.

Nigel could've asked her anything and she would've agreed.

She reminded herself that the closer she pulled herself to the mogul, the better her chances were to find the exact information she needed. On the other hand, taking on a longer project may prove to be dangerous…from all angles. Still, she would stay until she got the ammunition she needed on Miranda and then Sophie would have to go.

"How was your dinner?" Nigel asked.

Sophie glanced down to her plate and was shocked she'd been able to eat a bite, what with the guilt and nerves fighting for top spot in her belly.

"Fine," she lied with a smile. "Much better than

grabbing takeout and heading back to my apartment."

Her uptown penthouse was actually perfect. She'd spared no expense when looking for a short-term lease. She'd had to pay for the entire month, but she would be out long before that...she hoped.

The glass walls she had offered her a spectacular view of Central Park, and with the snow they'd had lately, every time she looked out her windows, she felt a little bit of giddiness. She didn't have snow in her part of Texas and the blanket of white always took her breath and inspired her for future designs.

"We can dine together every night if you prefer not to eat alone," he replied, placing his napkin on the table.

"This isn't a date."

"Of course not. You know I don't date employees." Nigel quirked a brow. "Did I imply it was?"

"Actually, yes."

He laughed and shrugged. "I like your company, both professionally and personally. You're not immune to all of this, either."

There went those nerves again. And when he'd toyed with the ends of her hair? Revved up all of her sexual urges with the simplest of ways. Still, he didn't get involved with his staff, or so he kept saying, and she couldn't throw away her virginity on a man she was lying to and essentially using.

Except, she wanted to. Mercy how she wanted to.

She was so out of her league here. The flirting, the charm… She was a complete innocent in every sense of the word.

"Dating would certainly complicate things," she finally stated. "I mean, I'm only working for you temporarily and for all you know I have a boyfriend back in Texas."

Nigel reached for her hand, stroked his thumb along the top of her knuckles, and stared directly into her eyes so intently that she'd swear he could see into her soul.

Oh, boy. He may keep saying he didn't date employees, but he hadn't said anything about making said employees ache with desire.

"If you have a man in Texas, then he's a fool for letting you come here alone."

Oh, that low British accent had her toes curling in her Ferragamo pumps. There went that belly flutter again.

"Do you hit on all of your employees?" she asked.

"I've never made a pass at any woman I worked with," he explained. "I've never wanted to."

Until now.

The words hovered between them and she wished she could ignore the blaring bells and red flags waving in her mind. If this were another time, another place, if she could show him her true identity and start over, then maybe this attraction could lead to something more.

But the harsh reality was she was only here to take down her ex-step-monster. She'd gone to drastic measures to do so and she couldn't get sidetracked now—not when she'd promised her brothers. And besides, how could they build anything real between them now? She couldn't keep up the facade forever, and the more deeply they got involved, the more betrayed he'd feel when he learned she'd been lying to him all along.

"I have to attend the CBN Awards Ceremony on Friday. I was going to go alone because it's not a big deal and I know this is last minute but…" That thumb continued to stroke her hand and he eased just a touch closer. "Join me."

"Nigel, I—"

"I'll send my personal stylist to your office tomorrow morning," he went on. "Choose anything you want and I'll make sure hair and makeup are informed you'll need their services. They'll come to you, so don't worry about that."

Was she living in some warped version of *Pretty Woman*? Turning into someone she wasn't and getting a makeover to go out and be draped on the arm of the hottest man she'd ever met?

If her brothers had any idea Nigel Townshend was hitting on her, or the way he kept looking at her and touching her, they'd have had her on the jet back to Texas before she could even say *Pretty Woman*.

"I'm not sure how it would look—my going to an awards show with you," she replied. "Especially since I'm new and we just started working more closely together."

Not to mention the fact if the cast of *Secret Lives* was there, Miranda would recognize her right off the bat. Glasses and blond hair would only cover so much.

"Won't you want to go with the ladies from the show?" she asked. "You know, like a united front?"

"This isn't a ceremony for them," he replied. "It's for directors, producers, creators. It's a small affair, but I'm expected to attend."

Miranda wouldn't be in attendance? He was offering up a free dress, hair, and makeup, and a night of schmoozing?

Beyond all of that, Sophie had never felt such a pull, such an instant bond to another man. How could she just ignore all of that? Yes, this was the worst possible timing considering the circumstances, but she was in the thick of things now, so…

Sophie smiled. "I'd love to go."

The smile that spread across Nigel's face had her wondering if she'd just sacrificed every part of her sanity…and her heart.

Six

"Okay, Nigel," Lulu said, as she stepped from her en suite. "I'll try to hint around to Fee about her wedding. I agree it would be amazing to make it a special episode of the show."

"Thanks, Lulu," Nigel replied. "I knew I could count on your support."

She disconnected the call and slid her cell into the pocket of her robe.

Lulu Shepard may be one of the stars on *Secret Lives*, but her life was crumbling. Her very best friend, the one she confided in and went to when she needed a trusted soul, was leaving the show.

Seraphina had found love and was moving to

Texas to begin her life. Lulu was happy for her, but selfishly she wanted her friend to stay in her life, as a constant, reassuring presence. Though she did love the idea of the wedding being aired for the world to see. The love Fee and Clint found should be shared and celebrated at any opportunity.

But after the wedding…what would Lulu do with Fee so far away? Their luncheons would be reduced to texts and occasional calls. Even now, Fee was away more than she was home, spending as much time as she could with Clint in between packing up her life in Manhattan. It was almost enough to make Lulu wish she'd stayed longer in Texas… But no, it was better that she'd left.

This show was such a huge part of her life and she loved every aspect of it. She truly had no idea what she'd do if the show failed or if she didn't have that constant in her life anymore.

The doorbell rang and Lulu glanced to the time. Nearly ten o'clock. Who would be stopping by this late?

Clearly someone the doorman knew, but he hadn't buzzed her to let her know, meaning it was either a neighbor or the guest was on the list to be allowed up unannounced.

That narrowed down her suspects to just a handful.

She crossed her penthouse and looked out the peephole. The one person she both wanted to see and wanted to avoid stood on the other side.

Kace LeBlanc.

She tightened the knot on her silky robe and pulled in a shaky breath as she slid the lock and opened the door.

"Kace."

Those warm brown eyes landed on her and she felt the jolt just as fiercely as if he'd reached out and touched her.

She'd done some reckless things with Fee and the cast of the show, but none had been as reckless as starting to lose her heart to Kace. The man was the opposite of her, he lived in Texas, he irritated the hell out of her… But she couldn't deny there was still something about him that turned her on in ways she couldn't explain.

She'd seen a different side of him when they'd helped clean up from the fires in Royal. He'd not been so cocky and arrogant. He'd been…strong, powerful, commanding in a ridiculously sexy sort of way as he'd worked to get things organized and put the town back in order.

And she'd ultimately given in to that attraction. Who could blame her? There was no way she could keep denying herself, denying him.

"What are you doing here?" she finally asked.

His eyes raked over her state of undress and she shivered once again. Who knew a stare could be so potent?

Kace took a step forward, urging her back until he was inside and could close the door behind him.

"I'm in town for business," he told her. "I was walking to my hotel and the next thing I knew, I ended up here."

"Without calling or texting?" she asked, irritated that he could get to her on every level. "That's rude, Kace, even for you."

He took one step closer. "Are you going to turn me away?"

Lulu crossed her arms to keep from reaching for him. "No. No, I'm not."

The smile that spread across his face had her wondering what the hell she was getting in to.

"Did I tell you how stunning you look tonight?"

Sophie didn't need the words. She could tell by the way Nigel kept close to her side, the way his eyes would roam over her as if he knew exactly what she looked like out of this sultry red dress that fit her every curve.

When she'd seen all of the options for her to try on, she'd fallen in love with this one immediately, unable to stop herself from imagining how Nigel would respond to the sight of her in it. He hadn't disappointed. She should've turned him down, she should've stayed focused on her task and not gotten swept up in all of the glitz and glamour and limo rides with a sexy man.

Yet here she sat in the back of his car as they maneuvered through the city streets. He shifted in his seat and his leg brushed hers, as if she needed the reminder of how close they'd been all evening.

Throughout the entire night, Nigel had constantly touched her in some way—his hand on her lower back to guide her, his thigh aligning with hers beneath the table at dinner, a simple hand holding hers as he led her to and from the car.

"There wasn't a man in that ballroom who wasn't mesmerized by you," he went on. "I'm glad you were my date."

"So this *was* a date?" she asked, trying to search his face as the flashes of the lights off the streets and buildings slashed across his features.

"What if it was?"

Be careful.

The voice rang through her head, but she ignored it. There was nothing careful about being this close, this attracted to the man she was deceiving.

She'd never misled a single person in her life and here she was lying to the one person she actually wanted to get to know on a personal level.

But there was so much chaos going on in her life, how could she even think about something personal with Nigel? Their lives were worlds apart and he didn't even know her real name.

"I thought you didn't get mixed up with employees," she countered.

He slid his fingertip along the slit in her skirt... the one that extended all the way up her thigh. Sophie shivered as her eyes darted from his hand to his face.

"I never have," he agreed, with a level gaze. "Maybe I've changed my mind...if you're interested."

Up and down that fingertip went. He touched her nowhere else, but she couldn't suppress the arousal that spiraled through her. She needed to put a stop to this... She'd needed to stop him long ago, such as when he'd asked her to join him for dinner or when he'd stared at her in the penthouse office like she was the most delectable thing and he was a starving man.

"Nigel—"

His finger stilled. "Should I stop?"

Sophie pursed her lips as a silent sparring battle took place between her awakened wants and common sense.

But she'd put her career ahead of her personal life for so long. Couldn't she just take what she wanted? Just this once? Who said she had to save herself for the right man? What if that perfect one never came along? What if Nigel *was* the right man?

"You're thinking," he murmured. "I can practically see you arguing with yourself."

"Sometimes I just want to ignore what's right, what's expected of me." Her thoughts spilled out before she could keep them inside. "Do you ever have that guilty feeling that you're being selfish?"

Nigel's eyes dropped to her lips. "Every decision I make is on purpose. So, no. I don't have regrets."

Of course, someone as powerful and confident as Nigel wouldn't second-guess his actions. He likely had his life all laid out to perfection with no worries of consequences.

Sophie had always prided herself on her own strength, but sitting in the back of a dark car with her faux boss had her willpower shrinking. Even before tonight, he'd mesmerized her and made her wish for and want more than she'd ever allowed herself.

Why couldn't this be easy? Why couldn't she have met him under different circumstances? Why did she have to choose between holding true to her legacy and the promise to her brothers and going after what she desperately wanted?

Before Sophie could say anything, the car came to a stop and moments later, her door opened. The driver extended his hand to assist her and as soon as she stepped out, she realized they weren't at her penthouse, but back at Green Media.

She glanced back to Nigel as he exited the vehicle.

"That will be all, James."

The driver got back into the car and drove away.

"How am I going to get home?" she asked.

Nigel smiled. "If that's where you want to go, I'll have him come back."

"And my other option?"

"Coming up to the penthouse with me."

She took one step toward him, silently telling him she wanted just that. She wasn't sure why he brought her here, maybe he wanted to do some work later, maybe he wanted her to feel like they were on neutral ground since they both worked here... she had no clue.

Her imagination went into overdrive and she wasn't so sure she was ready for more than this sexual banter and heavy tension. But if not now... when?

They were clearly attracted to each other and they were both adults. She was tired of always working. Even with her fake work she was working.

While she loved her job, it had always come ahead of her own personal life. Like now. Even her faux job was getting in her way.

Sophie adjusted her clutch beneath her arm and pulled in a shaky breath.

"I could use a drink first," she admitted, shivering against the cold.

Nigel removed his suit jacket and draped it around her shoulders. Now she was fully enveloped by his scent, his warmth. Another stepping stone on this path they'd started down together.

A glass of wine sounded good right about now.

Who knows, maybe they could start talking and she'd find more information on Miranda, because so far her search had turned up nothing useful. Wasn't that why she was here? To get some sort of proof that her stepmother swindled her way into the will and deceived Buck?

Or maybe Sophie was here at this moment to do something for herself. To finally give in and take what she'd denied herself for so long. Because right now, she wanted to be here for Nigel and absolutely nothing, or no one, else.

"A drink," he repeated with a crooked grin. "I can manage that."

She'd never been more aware of any man in her life than she was in that elevator on their way up to the penthouse. There was plenty of room, yet he stood at her side, with his hand beneath his jacket at the small of her back where her dress dipped low and exposed her bare skin.

That woodsy cologne of his had tantalized her all evening. She'd never been turned on by a man's scent before, but, well, everything with Nigel was becoming her first.

The door slid open and she stepped into the penthouse. As she walked through, the lighting automatically lit up her path. The view of the city below drew her to the wall of windows. The swirling snow shone bright as it caught the various lights from buildings and the streets below.

"I never thought I'd be so mesmerized by snow."

Nigel's dress shoes shifted across the hardwood floors. "You look good in the city. This life suits you."

If he only knew how much she missed her old self. Her boots and flip-flops, her long, flowy dresses. Pants were of the devil and she was so over them. Give her a nice maxi or A-line sheath any day over skinny jeans and tailored jackets.

She missed the ranch and wondered what all was going on now. She missed her French-inspired home in her luxurious gated community. And she desperately missed her own bed.

A flash of an image with Nigel in her bedroom pierced her thoughts. He could never be there. He could never know she was truly a Blackwell. If he ever discovered why she was truly here, he'd never forgive her and he'd never believe she hadn't set out to deceive him.

If he could have only known the real Sophie without this deception getting in the way...

"You prefer red or white?"

Sophie glanced over her shoulder to Nigel at the bar in the corner. She offered a smile and gripped the lapel of the jacket, pulling it tighter around her chest.

"I think you know by now I prefer white."

He picked up the stem he'd already poured. "Just making sure," he said, returning her smile.

As he made his way over to her, Sophie tried to

put her worries, her betrayal out of her mind. She took in the sight of her date bringing her a glass of wine, thought of how quickly he'd wrapped her in his jacket, remembered how he'd been impressed with her ideas and gave her credit for them without stealing them as his own when he very well could have.

Nigel was a noble man, a man she could easily fall for...was already falling for.

This date was going far beyond what she'd envisioned.

Date. She really shouldn't let that term settle in because actual dating wasn't possible for them. A date would imply there could be more, but other than attraction and flirting...this was all there could be.

Unless she was up front with him with as much as she could be and still not ruin her quest for the downfall of Miranda.

"I'm not naive," she told him as she took the glass. "I'm also not going to deceive you."

Well, not any more than she had to.

Nigel held onto his tumbler and raised his brows. "Is there something you think I've misunderstood?"

She pulled in a breath and took a sip of her wine before she exposed a very personal truth. "I've been focused on my career and trying to grow my design business, so my social life has taken a backseat."

More like it wasn't even in the car.

"I want to be the best at any job I do," she went on. "So dating hasn't exactly been on my radar."

"I'll take it as a compliment that you made an exception for me."

Sophie rolled her eyes. "You would," she laughed before pulling in a deep breath. "What I'm trying to say is that I realize you called this evening a date and I'm positive you brought me up here hoping we could extend our...um..."

"Oh, now you're shy?" he asked. "You've been so blunt and honest since you came to work for me. Don't stop now."

"Fine." She squared her shoulders and tipped her chin. "We've already agreed there's an attraction, so I won't pretend you don't hit every button for me."

"Is there a but?"

"But," she went on, "you need to know one vital piece of information before you decide anything else about me."

He took a sip of his own drink and took another step closer to her. "And what's that?"

"I've never been with a man before."

Seven

Nigel stared at Roslyn and waited for her to laugh or tell him she was joking. But those bright eyes continued to hold his and she didn't even offer a hint of a smile.

An innocent. He honestly didn't know any adult who was still a virgin. Yet the one woman he'd been craving for days—even though it sure as hell seemed much longer than that—stood before him as vulnerable as she could be. Quite the juxtaposition to her bold, confident personality in every other aspect of her life.

She hadn't had to tell him, yet she'd trusted him with her most personal piece of information.

"I totally understand if you want to end with the drinks and call your driver to come get me."

Without a word, Nigel took the glass from her hand and sat both of their drinks on the accent table. Turning back to face her, he stepped closer to her and framed her face until she had no choice but to look directly at him.

"I've said this before, but I've never met anyone like you."

Her eyes studied him. "I can't tell if that's a good thing or a bad thing."

"Good," he laughed. "Definitely good."

"So... I'm staying?"

His body stirred and he had to force himself to move slowly. He'd never had to worry about this before, but he found that her being a virgin wasn't a turn off at all...quite the opposite, actually.

"Everything from here on out is your call," he told her, grazing his thumb across her plump lower lip.

He'd never relinquished control of anything in his life, but found that's exactly what he wanted to do with Roslyn. He not only wanted her comfortable, he wanted to follow her lead, to learn with her as she expressed herself and explored her passion.

Nerves settled deep and he had to tamp down the anxiety over the thought that he was taking advantage. He wasn't about to do anything she didn't want, but he had questions.

"Were you that focused on work you didn't take time for yourself?"

"I want to make a name for myself," she told him. "Personal life could always come later."

Or now.

Nigel leaned in and slid his lips across hers. Her swift intake of breath and the increased pulse at the base of her throat only increased his need to make her feel everything she'd deprived herself of.

The fact that he was the first one to even make her think about giving herself up in such a way was more than an ego boost…it was a bloody treasure.

"So why are you here with me?"

She licked her lips and he knew the act stemmed from nerves and not some practiced ploy. "Because I can't help myself," she murmured honestly. "I've never felt drawn to someone the way I've been drawn to you. I know it's not right since you're my boss and I've tried to ignore what I feel."

Nigel eased the jacket from her shoulders and tossed it aside. "What do you feel?"

He tipped her head and braced one arm around her lower back to hold her firmly against him.

"Attracted, desired." Her eyes dropped to his mouth. "Aroused."

For someone so innocent, she knew all the right words to say. She raised her hand, hesitated, then placed it on the side of his face.

There was that hint of insecurity. He'd never seen

even an inkling of that in the office. She'd always been confident and strong. Even in the minor position she'd been hired for initially, someone like Roslyn was too big in life to be a simple consultant.

"Don't be afraid," he told her, even though fear pumped through him. He wanted everything to be perfect for her. Roslyn deserved more than for him to swipe off the top of his desk and lay her out.

She'd never done this before and he had to respect her reasons why…even if they were foreign to him.

Nigel took her hands in his and stepped back. Then he led her to the oversize leather sofa and urged her down. As she sat, those expressive eyes stared back at him. He'd have given anything to rip that excuse for a dress off her body and explore her tempting curves with his eyes, his hands, his mouth, but he didn't want to rush or frighten her.

Self-control was key here.

Roslyn started to reach for the top of his pants, but he pulled away. Confusion flashed across her face as she stared back up at him.

Nigel dropped to his knees in front of her, circling her waist with his hands, and leaning in to brush his lips across the swell of her breasts where her dress dipped.

"Trust me," he murmured over her heated skin. "Let me make you feel good."

"I'm feeling pretty good already," she sighed, settling deeper into the sofa.

The flare of her hips beneath his hands had him eagerly roaming down and pulling the skirt of her red dress back up over her shapely legs. He shifted his focus between her eyes and the dark skin he revealed inch by inch. He didn't want to miss a single part of her experience.

Roslyn stared down at his hands, her mouth open, her lids heavy. Desire looked good on her and he planned on making sure she knew just how desirable she truly was.

Anticipation pumped through him, knowing no other man had ever touched her in such a way. The experience seemed heightened, the intensity raised to a dizzying degree. He was too far gone, and from the little pants and sighs, so was she. Obviously she wanted this just as much as him.

Nigel glanced down to peek at the black lacy panties visible from beneath the slit of the skirt. He slid his thumb over the delicate material, right at the point where he knew she ached.

Her gasp had him smiling. So responsive, so passionate. She was utterly perfect, and he hadn't even pleasured her yet.

When the snug dress wouldn't move anymore, Nigel gripped her hips and tugged her into a half-laying position. Better. Now he could shift the dress a bit more and expose the rest of those lacy panties.

His breath left his lungs as he finally took her in from the waist down. He'd never seen a sexier sight and he ached to touch her, to taste her.

Roslyn's hands threaded through his hair as she continued to stare back at him. The want and need he saw looking back at him had Nigel ready to give her anything she wanted…and more.

Unable to wait a moment longer, he leaned down and slid his lips over her, where the lacy seam met skin. She trembled beneath his touch and Nigel continued to hold onto her hips as he explored her with his mouth.

Those fingers in his hair tightened, pulled, and only further aroused him. Roslyn had all this pent-up passion and he was about to make her come undone.

He curled his fingers over the scraps of material at her hips and slowly eased the panties down her legs. She still wore those bedroom heels and he most definitely wanted those to stay in place. He was a sucker for a woman in heels.

"Nigel," she whispered.

He stilled, raking his gaze up her body until he met her eyes. "You trust me?"

She bit her lip and nodded. Nigel slid one fingertip over her, earning him a soft moan.

He eased farther down, settling his shoulders between her parted legs. She continued to thread her fingers through his hair, as if she couldn't stop touching him. He was so damn aroused and turned on, but this moment, this night, was all about her. He never believed selfishness had any place in the bedroom and he sure as hell wasn't about to start now.

While he'd love nothing more than to shed this suit and show her exactly how much he wanted her, that would do Roslyn no good. He wanted her to see exactly how great this could be, how perfect her first sexual experience should feel.

No pressure, right?

His lips barely grazed her center and her hips bucked. The need for more had him sliding one finger into her.

Roslyn cried out and he absolutely loved the sounds she made…loved knowing he was the one making her come undone.

When he replaced his finger with his mouth, Nigel knew he'd never experience a sweeter, more erotic moment in his life. Roslyn moaned as she arched into his touch.

Nigel pleasured her until she gasped his name and fisted her fingers in his hair, pulling tighter than before. Her heels locked behind his back, the point of her shoe dug in and he didn't care one bit.

This. Was. Everything.

Roslyn had a passion that he'd never seen in another woman. She had an abandon that proved she wasn't ashamed to be herself, to expose the most intimate side of herself.

Nigel waited until her trembling ceased before he kissed her inner thighs and eased up. When he glanced down, he took a mental picture, never wanting to forget this for a second. Her hair had come undone, now spread all around her. Her eyes were closed, her mouth open, a sheen across her chest, her breathing rapid.

Roslyn looked exactly like what she was…a woman well loved.

But he had no clue what to do now. Nigel had never been in this situation before. He'd never been so bloody attracted to a woman, and a virgin at that. And she still was a virgin.

Damn it. He was more scandalous than the stars of his show. If anyone found out he'd taken his brand-new hire to bed, his reputation would be shattered. It would give weight to every doubt and reservation his family had expressed, every time they'd told him that New York wasn't his place and he should come home *where he belonged*. He'd built a life for himself here that he could be proud of— how could he risk throwing that all away?

And yet how could he resist this woman who had given him this beautiful gift? Besides, she was showing him such trust—surely he could show a little trust in return that everything would work out.

Nigel pushed aside any thoughts that didn't center around Roslyn. Because right now, and for the foreseeable future, all he wanted was to continue showing this woman just how much she was desired.

Eight

Sophie pulled in a shaky breath and attempted to sit up and right her dress.

They had just broken all the rules. This could hurt the business he loved so much and it could jeopardize her plan to protect her family's legacy. But she wasn't sorry this had happened. How could she be? Nigel had just pleasured her in the most intimate way and he hadn't even fully undressed her.

He slid his hands over her thighs, up to her waist, and pulled her forward.

"I don't know what to say," she muttered, feeling reality crash back down.

"You don't have to say anything," he replied with a naughty grin. "Believe me, this was my pleasure."

Speaking of...

"Don't you want—"

"Oh, more than you know." He cut her off with a low laugh that seemed to hold more frustration than humor. "But this was about you. I've wanted you since you stepped foot into my office. I can't resist you, Roslyn."

There it was. The reason she couldn't fully enjoy her first sexual experience. Nigel didn't even know her real name. Guilt and disappointment spiraled through her. She'd finally chosen to give herself to someone, and her pleasure had been robbed by her lies. She had nobody to blame but herself.

How could she let this go any further? Clearly Nigel cared for her on some level. He'd taken his time, he'd made love to her with his mouth, and now he looked as if he was perfectly content with nothing more.

Why couldn't she have met him before the deceit? Why couldn't she just tell him who she was and why she was here?

Because her brothers were counting on her and she couldn't let them down. Miranda had no right to take ownership of a family legacy that meant nothing to her anyway.

"I may be inexperienced," she told him. "But I'm not naive or dumb. You've got to be...frustrated."

Again, he let out a throaty laugh. "I'll admit to being a trifle uncomfortable."

His smile slowly faded and those lingering eyes continued to hold her in place. Another burst of arousal slid through her, coupled with fear of all the unknown components that made up this warped relationship.

At some point, this was all going to blow up in her face and they were both going to end up hurt. The longer she stayed, the more involved they became, the more Sophie knew there would be no good way for this to end.

Nigel sighed and came to his feet. He raked a hand over his mussed hair and stared down at her, then offered a soft smile.

"You look good spread out over my couch," he told her. "I've envisioned you several times, in several ways—spread across my bed, in my shower, on my desk."

Sophie adjusted her dress and stood, tugging the material down to cover her thighs. "You've been busy," she joked, though her nerves were even more out of control than they'd been before he'd pleasured her.

"I told you, I've never met a woman like you." He tucked a strand of hair behind her ear and raked his thumb over her chin. "Nobody has been able to distract me from work before and nobody has ever made me want to put them first in everything. You've put some spell on me."

Sophie swallowed, unable to form words to follow his declaration. This was getting too deep, too intimate... But she knew tonight was just a stepping stone for the future. She wasn't innocent enough to think they'd just stop here.

"I could say the same," she replied, still recovering from his touch. "I just didn't expect any of this."

She had to tell the truth where she could. Maybe he'd even turn out to be understanding. After all, he'd have to see that her attraction to Nigel had nothing at all to do with her plan to reveal Miranda for the ruthless gold digger Sophie believed her to be.

But what if he took it badly? What if he threw her out...and then called Miranda to tell her everything? She couldn't bring herself to risk it.

Lying to his face made her miserable. She'd never felt so guilty, so ugly. But she'd already started this and she would see it through.

"The new responsibilities I've given you have nothing at all to do with this attraction," he told her. "I need you to know that. In a very short time, you've proven to be a worthy asset."

Sophie smiled. "I didn't think you gave me an extra project to get in my pants. But I'm glad to know you find my ideas of value."

At least she could be a little proud of the effort

she'd put into this faux job. If she'd learned anything from her father, it was how to work hard no
matter the occupation.

She just wished her father would've thought more
of her and her brothers and shown some real care
toward them—in his life or in his death. Money and
assets aside, she didn't know why he wouldn't leave
them a part of his legacy. Why he would throw it
all at Miranda like she deserved more in her blingy,
snobby life. The woman mainly stayed in New York
with her friends and outgoing lifestyle. Her place
in Royal was just a getaway.

Even though Sophie and her father had had a
strained relationship, having everything removed
from her life where he was concerned seemed so
final, so heartbreaking. Like she just had to sever
any ties she had with him. He was her father, she
still loved him and she had nothing of his to hold
on to.

"I'm glad you decided to go to the ceremony with
me tonight," Nigel interrupted her thoughts, reaching for her hand and lacing his fingers with hers.
"You may not believe me, but I typically go alone."

Sophie tipped her head. "I do find that hard to
believe."

Nigel wrapped his arms around her, pulling her
in closer to his solid, powerful body. "And I find it
hard to believe no man has captured your attention
or your heart yet."

She stilled. "Is that what you're after? My heart?"

Nigel slid his hands over her backside and squeezed. "I'm not looking to fall in love, not when I'm busy building an empire and a name for myself. But I wouldn't mind some companionship while you're in town."

"A fling?" she asked.

"That's such a juvenile, crass term."

He slid his lips over hers, so softly she had to grip onto his shoulders to keep herself grounded in the face of the tenderness.

Sophie eased back and studied his face. "Then what do you mean?"

"There's no reason we can't enjoy each other's company," he told her. "I like being with someone whose body isn't the only sexy part. You're a match to my business mind and that's refreshing in this industry. You challenge me to be better and that's quite an admirable trait."

Again, she was flattered he found her useful and formidable, and that he noted she was smart. That meant so much to her because she did pride herself on being an educated woman.

"Is that all you want my company for?" she asked.

"Hell, no." He slid his hands up over the curve of her hips to settle at her waist. "I want to be the man who continues to awaken this inner vixen. I want to be the man who shows you what intimacy can be. I'm a jealous bastard and I hate the thought of any other man being any of those things to you."

Sophie shivered at his commanding, authoritative tone. She'd learned vital information about Nigel tonight: he was a giving lover and he was a force to be reckoned with. As strongly independent as she prided herself on being, she couldn't ignore his advances and she didn't want to.

But why couldn't she enjoy Nigel's company while she was here? She was a grown woman and didn't need to make excuses for going after what she wanted. She wasn't going to hurt him or Green Room Media. All Sophie wanted to do was find some juicy dirt on Miranda and then she'd be on her way.

But Sophie needed to find the scoop sooner rather than later. Her week was nearly up, and she had nothing to take back to Texas other than the best sexual experience she'd ever had. She wasn't ready to go, the thought of leaving had knots of anxiety and tension balling up within her.

Emotionally, she couldn't afford to keep up this charade. Even though she'd devised a sneaky scheme, she truly wasn't a ruthless person and she didn't like stooping to this level. But, if she left, she'd be leaving Nigel and she wasn't ready.

"You seem to still be thinking."

Nigel's words cut into her thoughts and she re-directed her attention to him.

"Maybe I wasn't persuasive enough," he added, bending down to run those talented lips along her exposed neck.

Sophie dropped her head back and curled her fingertips into his shoulders. Did anyone ever say no to this man?

"I'm yours," she muttered, helpless against his persuasion. "For as long as I'm here."

She didn't know if she should hurry and get out before she got hurt or take her time and enjoy the ride.

"We haven't received confirmation of your plus one."

Nigel pinched the bridge of his nose and closed his eyes. He could handle the cat fighting and nit-picking of the ladies from *Secret Lives* without breaking a sweat, but when it came to his grand-mother, he somehow resorted to a child being scolded.

"I haven't sent in my plus one, yet," he replied, blowing out a sigh.

"Yes, I'm aware. Hence the nature of my call."

Dame Claire Worthington never failed to choose sharp, witty words and there wasn't a soul in the family, or anywhere else in Cumbria, that dared cross her. In addition to being strict and demanding, she was also loving, loyal, respected…and that's why he hated letting her down.

Nigel turned from the wintery view of the city to face the leather sofa…the one he'd had Roslyn spread out on just last night. He'd told himself that he'd come up here to think and get away from the office for the day, but perhaps he just wanted to return to the scene of the best night of his life.

He had no clue what was happening with his new temporary employee, but he knew he wanted more from her…professionally and personally. Why couldn't he have both? He made the bloody rules and owned the company. He wanted her to stay on permanently, not just because he wanted her in his bed, but because she'd already brought so much to Green Room Media. Workplace romances happened all the time—there had to be some kind of protocol they could follow to keep everything scandal-free.

"Nigel."

"Yes, yes," he stated, shifting his attention back to his grandmother. "I know. Plus one."

"The RSVP was due in by today. I'm sure it slipped your mind with as busy as you are with your city life, so that's why I called. You can just tell me you'll be bringing a date to your sister's wedding and I'll make sure catering gets the accurate number."

As if an inaccurate count of his one date, or lack of, would throw off the filet Oscar-style menu. His grandmother made it no secret he was only getting older and that she disapproved of the fact that he still hadn't settled down, let alone started working on producing the next generation of little Townshends.

His grandmother was old school and British... there was no arguing with her and she damn well knew it. But for all that, she certainly wasn't the pearl-wearing, tea-sipping elderly woman. She worked hard all her life, raised her children without a nanny and ran their horse farm alongside her husband. She understood his reasons for wanting to build his own empire and the move to NYC, but she wasn't backing down on his settling soon to start a family.

"You are cutting this close," she added. "The wedding is next week, you know."

"I'm aware."

His sister was marrying the love of her life...or so she said. They'd chosen Valentine's Day as their wedding day, which was just a little too cutesy for him, but she hadn't asked his opinion.

Nigel had met his soon-to-be brother-in-law a handful of times when he'd gone home and the guy seemed like he'd fit into the Townshend family perfectly. But Nigel was in no hurry to bring home a woman. It would take someone special to get him ready to introduce her to the rest of the clan.

An image of Roslyn flashed through his mind.

No. Hell, no. First of all, when he brought a date, they wouldn't expect her to be someone from the office. Second, he couldn't bring Roslyn because... well...

Why not? She would actually be the perfect candidate. She was poised, she could definitely hold her own and there was nobody else he'd want on his arm.

Nigel couldn't prevent the smile that spread across his face. His family would have no way of knowing Roslyn was from the office. If she came as his plus one, it would give him another opportunity to get to know her on a deeper level. He wasn't ready for that commitment his grandmother was after, but spending more time with Roslyn would give him more insight to her. A fake relationship for the sake of his family wouldn't hurt anything, right?

After that, he could explain they broke things off and nobody would have to know.

That is, if Roslyn went along with this crazy plan.

"And for pity's sake, wear a tie," Dame Claire scolded. "I know you have your own style, but this is a black-tie affair."

"Yes, ma'am." Ideas rolled through his mind on how to approach Roslyn with his proposal. "I promise I won't do anything to embarrass you or the family."

"Oh, please," she chided. "Nothing embarrasses me, but I do have standards. I expect you and your date to be here no later than Wednesday. The wedding is Saturday."

"I'll be there," he vowed.

"You *both* will be here," she corrected.

Nigel laughed. Of course she'd assume he was bringing someone simply because she said so. He told her to give everyone his love before he disconnected the call.

He stared at the phone another second and finally shot off a text before he could think better of it.

Going up against a persnickety, hardheaded old grandmother called for drastic measures.

Meet me at the office penthouse.

He hit Send, then quickly added another text.

I need a favor.

It was Saturday night, so maybe she was out on the town, but he didn't think so. Roselyn worked hard and seemed to put her career above socializing. He didn't want to discuss his family's drama and wedding issue via text. And he just wanted to see her…the wedding was just the perfect excuse.

Nigel didn't want Roslyn to think he was a complete jerk who only wanted to get her undressed. He'd meant what he'd said when he told her that he respected her and planned to take his time.

Time would prove to be the ultimate foreplay, especially since she'd already said yes to his advances. And a trip to his home? He couldn't wait to take her back to the place where he had grown up, where he'd dreamed. He'd continue to charm her with the grand estate of Shrewsbury Hall. The home itself rivaled Buckingham Palace with all the rooms, windows, ornate architecture and decor.

Roslyn would love his childhood home if he could get her there. He couldn't imagine any interior designer not falling in love with the rich history and all the stories behind each room and heirloom.

Nigel had to talk her into being his plus one first. Coming off their encounter last night, he hoped fate was in his favor.

Nine

"Meet your family?"

Sophie knew getting physically involved with Nigel was risky, both to her heart and her mind, but flying all the way to Cumbria, England, to be his plus one at his sister's wedding? And for Valentine's Day?

That was more than just taking a step in a dangerous direction—it was practically bungee jumping off a cliff. Meeting the family, attending a wedding that would equate to something from royalty and pretending to be his girlfriend for the sake of duping his family?

More lies might just do in her mental state and she wasn't sure she could keep all of them straight.

"I know this is out of nowhere," Nigel stated, raking a hand through his hair, clearly stressed.

She'd only known him a short time, but she'd never seen him this flustered. Clearly he was in a bind and wasn't any more comfortable asking her than she was being invited. She also had to assume that he wouldn't have come to her had he'd had another choice.

"My grandmother is quite persistent," he added, his dark eyes pleading with her.

"But, what about my job here?" she asked, still reeling from the out-of-the-blue request. "I mean, what will everyone think? First I'm hired as a consultant, then I'm put in charge of heading up the marketing for the wedding episode that may or may not happen, then I go to an award ceremony with you and now a family wedding back at your home?"

Her mind was spinning just saying all of this out loud. Talk about a whirlwind experience. But the biggest issue for her was the thing she didn't dare say aloud—between getting swept up with Nigel and his charm and sex appeal, and her inability to deny him anything, she was running out of time to uncover information on Miranda. Every angle she'd tried ended up a dead end. Everyone she spoke to absolutely loved the woman.

"I know it looks crazy... It *is* crazy," he amended, reaching for her hands. "Nobody here has to know about where we're actually going. I can say I have you going on a trip to scout potential locations for the show."

More lying. For someone who used to pride herself on honesty, she'd fallen down the rabbit hole of deceit and she wasn't sure she'd find her way back out anytime soon.

If she went away with him, Sophie knew they'd pick up where they'd left off the other night... That both thrilled and terrified her. She'd never wanted anyone the way she wanted Nigel and that was what scared her most. How could she ever let him go?

Nigel's strong hands held hers as he continued to stare at her, imploring her with his eyes.

"How long will we be gone?" she asked.

A toe-curling smile spread across his face. "Five days."

Five days in an English countryside estate with a man she was quickly falling for, during which she'd have to pretend to be his girlfriend so his family would get off his back. Seriously, what could go wrong?

Sophie had lied to get to this point and now she was taking this acting skill on an international tour. What would her brothers think when she told them about this venture?

Maybe she should keep this part to herself. She didn't want to use Nigel. That part kept niggling at her. She may be lying in her position here, but she wasn't lying about her growing feelings or attraction. She wasn't that good of an actress. But all of these emotions were completely unexpected and causing issues she hadn't planned on.

"I don't want to pressure you," he told her. "I just didn't want to ask anyone else."

The fact he trusted her with meeting his family and only added to her shame. He was being so transparent with his life with her, as far as she knew, and she was a complete phony.

Yet she couldn't say no. She wanted to spend more time with the man who made her wish this were all real. He made her daydream about a real relationship, a real attraction…a real affair instead of one based on lies.

"I'll do it," she told him. "I'll go to England."

Nigel's shoulders relaxed as he stepped closer her and gripped her hands to his chest. "You will love my home and my family. Dame Claire can be overwhelming at times, but she does everything out of love."

Sophie wasn't sure how she'd deal with a large, loving family and a doting grandmother…especially one with a title. Sure, she and her brothers were close, and she'd loved her her mother, but the relationship with her father just left her feeling broken.

What would her life be like if she had a close relationship with her father? Maybe the outcome of the will would've been different and Sophie and her brothers would have had their legacy given to them.

She only had her brothers now and they were depending on her. Even though Kellan had said she could come home, she didn't want to let them down. She wanted to be the one to make everything right. She wanted to give them back what had been taken away.

"What should I pack for this wedding?" Sophie asked, ignoring the blaring horns and red flags in her head.

Nigel quirked a brow. "I've got everything covered. My jet will be ready to go Wednesday morning and your dresses and jewelry will be on board."

And Sophie fell just a little deeper into this *Pretty Woman* scenario.

Central Park was absolutely gorgeous in the winter. Freezing, but breathtaking and so picturesque.

Sophie huddled deeper into her coat as she walked along the curved path through the park. The brisk air gave her a freshness that she didn't find in Texas heat. Besides, she'd wanted to get out of the office and take a much-needed break.

She'd tried calling Vaughn, but she'd only gotten his voice mail. She stopped at a park bench that had been cleaned off and took a seat, pulling out her phone to call Kellan.

She had to tell them what she'd be doing, but she'd been stalling, struggling with her guilt. In all of this snowballed mess, she had to be honest with someone. She couldn't exactly leave the country without letting her brothers know. She respected and loved them too much to lie… She'd done enough lying as it was.

Sophie dialed and wrapped her arm around her midsection to hold in the warmth of her coat. Kellan answered on the first ring.

"There's my favorite spy."

Sophie inwardly groaned, hating the nickname, even though this had all been her idea. "Good to hear your voice, too."

"Found out anything yet?"

"I'm getting closer," she stated, which was partially true. She was actually going to a meeting later with two members from the camera crew. If anyone knew about behind the scenes shenanigans, it would be them.

"I hope to have some information within the next few days," she added. "But I called to tell you that I have to do a bit of traveling. I'll still check in and keep my eyes and ears open, but… I'm going out of the country."

"Out of the country?" he repeated. "How does that fit into the plan when Miranda is going to be in New York for filming?"

Yeah, she was still trying to figure that out herself. In her original plan, she would have already left New York by now with the sought-after evidence in hand. As it was, she would have to dodge

Miranda if she popped into the office, but Sophie had seen the upcoming shooting schedule and there was no reason for Miranda to be at Green Room Media for the next few weeks.

"I can't do anything to raise suspicions," she defended. "I was asked to travel, so that's what I'm doing."

Swirls of snow fluttered around and mesmerized Sophie as she clutched the cell. For someone so accustomed to heat, she really was enjoying her time in NYC during the winter. Maybe she should visit more often. Perhaps she should even incorporate some of her videos here for inspiration... Well, once she could go back to being Sophie Blackwood, posh interior designer and not Roslyn Andrews, temporary consultant and wannabe mistress to Nigel Townshend.

"And going out of town is a direct order from the boss?" Kellan joked.

"Pretty much," she muttered, as die-hard runners braved the cold and jogged by. "Listen, it's only for five days and I promise I haven't lost sight of the prize."

"I'm sure you haven't. But, Darius said that Miranda invited him to Blackwood Hollow. I don't know what she has up her sleeve."

Sophie gripped her coat and the cell as dread settled into her belly. "He's coming there?" she exclaimed.

Darius Taylor-Pratt was their half sibling…a secret revealed after their father had passed. Even in death, her father continued to work his controlling hands in their lives.

"Apparently," Kellan replied. "She may be trying to pit him against us, but I'll keep my eye on things here. Don't worry."

"What the hell is she plotting?" Sophie muttered.

Frustration and confusion settled in alongside her guilt and she wondered if any of them would come out of this entire situation unscathed. And all because her father had been selfish or blinded by his young ex-wife and decided none of his children deserved their legacy.

Miranda sure as hell didn't deserve it, either. Buckley had been twenty-six years older than his bride. Why else would a beautiful young socialite marry a wealthy older man if not for the money she could get out of him? Miranda made no apologies for liking the finer things and Sophie knew the woman was just gathering a nest egg for the rest of her lavish life. And now she was pulling in Darius.

Sophie hated sounding spoiled and the issue truly didn't come down to money, but the fact Miranda just didn't deserve a dime of what should have been theirs. She didn't deserve the family home that held so many memories of Sophie's childhood. Sophie's brothers deserved to keep the estate, to pass down to their children one day.

"Does Vaughn know Darius is coming?"

"Yeah. We talked this morning. You know he doesn't like all this family drama, but he does want to know what's going on."

Sophie still didn't know why her father had never confessed there was another heir. Maybe he'd wanted them to find out after his death so he wouldn't have to deal with the questions, the repercussions. Or maybe he had wanted them to all be in an upheaval, perhaps pitting against each other. She truly had no idea what his ultimate plan had been for his children.

Sophie came to her feet and sighed. "Don't keep me out of the loop just because you're worried. I'm doing this grunt work and I deserve to be included as soon as you know anything."

"I promise to call you when I learn more," he vowed. "So, where are you going that's taking you away on business?"

Sophie didn't want to lie anymore. She was tired of it. Even though she knew she'd take backlash from Kellan and Vaughn, she had to be up front, because that's what she expected from them.

"Cumbria."

"What the hell for?"

Sophie cleared her throat and made her way back down the path. "Nigel is taking me for his sister's wedding."

"Excuse me?"

"You heard me."

"Damn it, Sophie. You're getting in too deep there. You need to just come home and we'll figure out something else. Traveling with Nigel Townshend to his home is a bad, bad idea."

Sophie bit the inside of her cheek, trying to quickly come up with the right words to reply, but Kellan beat her to it.

"Oh, no. Don't tell me you're sleeping with your fake boss."

"I'm not sleeping with him." *Not yet.* "He asked me to be his date because his grandmother is always on his back about not settling down. He figured if I went, they would at least leave him alone for a few days and he could enjoy his sister's celebration without getting hassled."

"Uh-huh. And you're telling me he's not interested in you?"

Oh, he was more than interested. Her body still tingled from just how interested Nigel Townshend was. There was nothing about her feelings for Nigel that she'd be sharing with her well-meaning brothers.

"Listen, I know what I'm doing and I'm a big girl. You worry about finding the scoop on our long lost sibling and I'll work on Miranda."

"I don't give a damn about Miranda right now," Kellan growled. "You can't get caught up in a love affair with Nigel. You're vulnerable, Soph. You're grieving and totally out of your element. Besides, Miranda will know what you're up to if she catches you anywhere near her showrunner."

"Stop worrying about my mental state. I'm fine," she assured him, even though she was worried herself. "And nobody is going to catch me. I barely recognize myself in the mirror with all this blond hair and these glasses."

It was true. She missed her dark hair. The blond did horrid things to her skin tone, but a dye job was worth the sacrifice if she could get some blackmail material on Miranda.

She might come across as all mama bear on the screen, doting on her costars and always trying to help, but nobody was that squeaky clean and wholesome. There had to be some proof that Miranda had done something underhanded to get the Blackwood money—something that would justify getting the will thrown out. Sophie wasn't sure how she could make this work to their advantage, but she had to try. No way was she giving up her childhood home that easily. If they could just get Miranda out of Royal for good, they could all move on to the next chapter of their lives. They hadn't gotten along with the woman when she'd been married to their father, so now that he was gone, there was no reason for her to stick around.

"I'm heading back to work," she told her brother.

"Keep in touch and don't make me beg for information."

She disconnected the call and made her way back to Green Room Media. She had a meeting to get to, a trip to prepare for and a stepmother to bring down.

All in a day's work.

Ten

Nigel settled into his seat as the jet taxied down the runway. He glanced at Roslyn, trying to figure out why she'd been so quiet and reserved on the way to the airport and since boarding.

Maybe he'd been too demanding by asking her to be his date. Maybe she'd felt pressured, like her job would be on the line if she refused. That wasn't the type of man he was, nor was it the type of man she deserved. He wanted her to know she mattered, she was valued. Not someone he considered disposable if she didn't comply with his wishes. And certainly not who could be bought.

Bloody hell. Since when did he try so hard to

impress a woman? He actually cared what Roslyn thought of him. Oh, he'd always prided himself on caring for his dates, his relationships, but no other woman had impacted him like Roslyn.

He admired her talents, her brilliance, and he couldn't ignore the sexual pull, the desire and passion he'd witnessed. The combination continued to make him wonder if there was something else smoldering beneath the surface…and he couldn't wait to explore.

Bringing Roslyn to his family's estate was risky, but hell, he'd taken risks his entire life… Why stop now when the reward could be so memorable and thrilling?

When the plane lifted, Roslyn gripped the seat and closed her eyes. A minimal act, but one that hinted at why she'd been so closed off since they'd boarded. Well, he'd finally found her flaw. He had honestly wondered if she was too good to be true… and if fear of flying was her only drawback, he was in real trouble.

Nigel didn't want a commitment or love or anything crazy long-term, but he enjoyed Roslyn and couldn't help but want to see where all this went.

He came to his feet and crossed the cabin to the other white sofa, taking a seat, and her hand. He squeezed, earning him a quick glance.

"What was that for?" she asked.

"You looked like you needed it. Why didn't you tell me you were afraid of flying?"

Roslyn lifted a shoulder and glanced down to their joined hands. "Pride? Fear of admitting I'm flawed? It's silly, actually. I mean, flying is the safest form of travel, or so the saying goes."

Nigel shifted in his seat and took both of her rigid hands in his. "Relax," he told her. "I've never been in a crash yet."

Roslyn rolled her eyes and gave a half grin.

"That's better," he murmured with a smile. "But, seriously, having a fear is nothing to be ashamed of. Why didn't you ask me to sit with you and hold your hand?"

"I've never asked anyone to hold my hand when I've been afraid," she countered. "Talk about humiliating."

"Everybody is afraid of something."

She quirked her brow and leveled his gaze. "And tell me what your fear is? Besides your grandmother."

Nigel laughed, but she wasn't far from the mark. He'd never discussed his true anxieties or insecurities with anyone before.

"Failing my family," he finally admitted. "They were all stunned when I wanted to move to New York and start my own brand and work in television. I need this show to continue to succeed not just for me but for them. And then there's my personal side.

Settling down, marrying, and starting the next generation of little Townshends is actually expected of me and I know my family is disappointed that I've waited this long. I could always find a woman and start a family, but that's not what I want. My parents were married a long time before my mother passed from a stroke. I want love. I'm just not sure when it will find me. I'm just so swamped with work and growing the brand."

Nigel stopped himself before he went on too much. He already sounded like a fool for believing in love. Roslyn had already said she wasn't sure the emotion truly existed and he wasn't so sure there was someone out there for him, either.

At what point should he give up and just find a woman he'd want to be the mother of his children? Did he actually have to love her in a way old romances said a husband should love a wife? What was even normal these days, anyway?

"Family really means that much to you."

Roslyn's murmured words pulled him back.

"Family is everything," he stated. "That's why I'm going to all this trouble to bring a date."

Her wide smile made her eyes sparkle. "And here I thought it was because you couldn't stand being away from me."

Nigel moved closer, settling his hands on either side of her hips until she had her back pressed against the leather couch.

"That, too," he said before he slid his mouth over hers.

She moaned against his lips, sliding her hands over his shoulders and threading her fingers through his hair. Just the simplicity of her touch had his arousal pumping through him. He had to remind himself that she was still innocent, but he also couldn't ignore how passionate she was.

When Roslyn arched that curvaceous body against his, Nigel slid his hands beneath the hem of her silky blouse and found warm satiny skin.

Roslyn tore her mouth from his and dropped her head back, his name coming out on a whisper from her lips.

"Tell me what you want," he demanded.

He wasn't going to do anything she wasn't comfortable with, but he wanted her more than he wanted his next breath…and they certainly had plenty of time on this flight for him to show her just how much he needed her.

"Tell me," he repeated, easing back to watch her face, to look for any hesitation that might indicate she wasn't ready for more.

Her eyes met his and she smiled…and his body responded. There was nothing in her eyes but hunger, desire and anticipation.

His hands shook as he slid her shirt up and over her head. When he tossed it to the side and reached for the straps of her lacy black bra, she reached up and framed his face with her hands.

"You're nervous," she stated with a soft smile. "That's adorable."

Adorable. Not a word anyone used to describe him since he'd probably been a toddler.

And nervous? Nigel wasn't about to admit any such thing…no matter how true the statement. They both needed this. They both had been dancing toward this moment since she sashayed into his office in those hip-hugging jeans and killer heels, dazzling him with her beauty and impressing him with her knowledge and her mind.

Instead of answering, he dipped his head to graze his lips over the swell of her breasts just above the outline of that sexy-as-hell bra.

Roslyn eased down as he reached behind her back and unhooked the garment. She jerked it from her arms and lay on her back, staring up at him, her eyes silently pleading for him to take her.

Definitely no hesitation here. This woman knew what she wanted, knew *whom* she wanted. Nigel may not understand why she'd waited so long to give herself to a man, but he was damn happy she'd chosen him.

He didn't know what this said about her true feelings, but he couldn't analyze that right now. He wanted her and she sure as hell wanted him.

With her blond hair all fanned out around her

and her body completely exposed from the waist up, Nigel didn't hesitate to remove the rest of her clothes, including her shoes. Once she laid bare beneath him, he came to his feet and made quick work of shedding his own things.

There were certainly perks to owning your own jet. Privacy being the key.

The way her eyes raked over him had Nigel hurrying even more. He procured protection from his wallet and covered himself before settling over her.

Her hands trembled as she slid her fingertips up his arms and over the curve of his shoulders.

"Looks like we're both nervous," she told him with a shaky smile.

This might as well have been his first time, too, because he did not want to screw this up. He wanted Roslyn to experience everything she deserved and more. Her satisfaction hinged on his every touch, his every move. Everything that happened here would be with her forever…and he knew this experience would be lasting for him, too.

Believing in someone was key in his life and he knew he had her trust if she had decided to give her virginity to him. The idea humbled him and made his confidence grow even deeper toward her.

Nigel was about to ask again if she was okay, but her knees came up on either side of his hips and she wrapped her legs around his waist. Nigel leaned down and covered her body, her mouth, still without joining them completely.

Taking his time was what he should have been doing, but all Nigel wanted to do was be one with her, to finally feel her heat and know her pleasure… to take everything she was willing to give.

Later they could explore. Between his own wants and her arched body and soft moans, Nigel knew they were both just as eager.

He lifted his head slightly, wanting to see every emotion she displayed as he slid into her.

Roslyn didn't disappoint.

Her mouth dropped open a second before she bit her lip, her lids fluttered shut, and she tipped her head back, pressing her breasts into his chest.

She. Was. Perfect.

Nigel moved carefully at first, more than aware of each sound or expression she made. They settled into a rhythm so effortlessly, as if they'd done this before…or as if they were meant to be.

The thought was silly, but there was no other way to describe the manner in which they fit and moved so beautifully.

She whispered his name on a plea as the rhythm of her hips quickened. Nigel followed her lead. She may lay beneath him, but all control was in her hands.

Roslyn's fingernails bit into his back as her climax took over. She arched, tightened her knees against his hips, and let out a cry of passion. Never before had he seen anything so erotic, and yet vulnerable.

Her abandon had him losing control even further and following her into his own release. Nigel gripped her hips and slid his mouth over hers to connect them in every way possible.

The hum of the engines and the heavy breathing in his ear were the noises in the cabin as his body came down from its high.

Nigel eased up, glancing at Roslyn who had the widest smile on her face, her eyes completely locked onto him.

"If you were trying to distract me from flying, you did a hell of a job."

Nigel laughed and pulled away from her, taking her hands to bring her up to his side.

"Well, since we have several more hours, I say we take this to the back bedroom so I can make sure you are completely relaxed."

Roslyn came to her feet and held out her hand. "Show me the way."

Eleven

Cumbria, England, was exactly like Sophie had imagined. Rolling snow-covered hills and little cottages dotted the landscape alongside the curvy road. The entire trip from the airstrip toward the Townshend estate was picturesque and she couldn't keep her eyes off the scenery. It was like being transported back into another time. One where life was simple and carefree. Much like the life she enjoyed back in Royal.

Perhaps she and Nigel weren't so different after all. He'd admitted how protective he was of his family, and he was clearly going to great lengths to please them…something she could totally relate to.

More and more she was seeing how compatible they were.

After that memorable plane ride, it was a wonder she could focus on anything but her tingling body. She couldn't stop herself from a constant replay of every single arousing touch. Those hours only pulled her in deeper to his world, making her want more, making her wish things were different.

Nigel reached over to take her hand and gave a gentle squeeze. "Nothing to worry about. My family will love you. We just have to pretend like we're in love."

She didn't even know how to unpack that whole statement, but she should at least attempt.

Nervous? She had far surpassed nervous when it came to meeting his family. His grandmother went by Dame for crying out loud.

And pretend? Yeah, she'd gotten that down pat and honestly deserved some Oscar for her performance.

Love? No, there was no love here. A good healthy dose of lust and sex, but not love. She couldn't allow herself to think along those lines because she was already falling, and at some point, she'd have to guard her heart from tumbling completely out of her control. She just didn't know where to draw the boundary lines.

"Do you want to talk about what happened on the

plane?" she asked as she turned from the postcard-worthy view to face him.

He steered the car around another sharp turn before flashing her a grin. "What do you want to talk about? I had a great time. Best flight of my life."

She wondered how many times he'd used that bedroom for other women he whisked off around the world. Jealousy had no place here, after all she was lying to him and they'd made no promises to each other. Still, she couldn't help where her mind wandered.

"Maybe I should have brought you on my plane sooner," he joked.

Sophie got a nasty pit in her belly. "Do you seduce many women on your private jet?"

"Don't go there," he growled. "I'm not a playboy like the tabloids want people to believe and I certainly don't seduce women in my jet."

"You had my clothes off before we reached cruising altitude," she countered. "You seemed pretty experienced."

"I haven't been a monk, but I swear that I have not taken any other woman to bed on my plane."

He sounded so sincere and Sophie really had no reason to disbelieve him. But the whens and wheres of his former affairs weren't really the issue here. Of course, he'd had women and relationships before her. He was a sexy, powerful man. Good grief, they weren't even in a relationship and she already had the unhealthy girlfriend mentality. They'd had sex and she was his pretend girlfriend for the rest of the week. Sounded simple enough, right?

But nothing was simple about her emotions or sex. If she'd thought she was falling for him before, the intimacy on the plane had only exacerbated the issue. Now she didn't know if her feelings stemmed from the man she finally gave herself to or if they came from the fact he truly was a genuine guy and not the playboy the media played him out to be.

Any other thoughts or words died in her throat as Nigel turned into a long drive where the grounds were surrounded with tall evergreens covered with a blanket of crisp white snow.

As he turned the last curve of the drive, the trees opened up to reveal a vast two-story brick-and-stone home. There seemed to be windows everywhere and juts of bay windows on both floors. Sophie imagined many reading nooks in those bays.

The home looked old, but not unkempt. The estate went right along with her original impression of the town—everything about this place was like she'd stepped back in time. She couldn't wait to explore the inside, get inspired for even more future designs, and learn of the history behind such a manor.

A large pond sat in front of the home and she could only imagine summertime here with the grounds blooming with colorful flowers. But even with the freshly fallen snow, the estate was breathtaking.

She'd uploaded some old material to her YouTube channel for the next month so she didn't have to worry about keeping up while she was undercover. But she would certainly be taking mental notes from this place for ways to incorporate new and old into any living area.

"Welcome to Shrewsbury Hall," Nigel told her as he circled the drive and pulled to the front entrance.

She'd heard him say that name before, but seeing the vast home made her realize it was certainly worthy of such an upstanding title. And she'd thought her family had money. This place could hold three of her own French provincial home. The mansion also made her father's ranch estate seem small.

A man in a wool coat and hat immediately came out and opened her door. Sophie pulled her coat around her chest and thanked him.

Nigel came around the car and shook the man's hand. "Thank you, William."

"Glad to have you back home, Sir Nigel."

Sir. Of course, he'd be addressed as such.

"It's good to be here." Nigel nodded toward the home. "Is everyone inside?"

"Dame Claire is waiting on you with bourbon and some snacks. She figured you'd be hungry after your flight and would need to relax with a drink."

"You mean she's ready to grill my girlfriend and me?" Nigel asked.

"That, too, sir."

Sophie was still reeling from the *girlfriend* comment when Nigel took her hand and led her up the stone steps to the front entrance. The architecture alone was drool-worthy and Sophie couldn't wait to see the interior. She could only imagine the videos she could shoot from here…if she were actually here as herself and had the opportunity to do such things.

She missed her design shoots, but since going undercover, she'd had to back off just a bit. She still replied to comments and answered her DMs on her social media accounts, but she was itching to get back to new material…and Shrewsbury Hall was the absolute perfect backdrop.

Too bad she wasn't here as Sophie Blackwood, interior designer.

Hell, she wasn't even here as Roslyn Andrews, consultant. She was here as an imposter of an imposter. Good grief. It would be a miracle if she didn't need therapy after this entire ordeal.

And after the hit to her mental state—and, inevitably, to her heart—she had better find some seriously juicy dirt on Miranda once she returned to New York.

"From what you've said before, I wouldn't have taken your grandmother for the bourbon type," Sophie muttered as they reached the door. "I assumed tea and cookies, or biscuits as you call them."

Nigel laughed. "Don't try to stereotype her. You'll never find a box that fits the personality of Dame Claire Worthington."

Sophie didn't know whether to be afraid or amused, but before she could decide, Nigel opened the double doors and swept her inside.

All air caught in her lungs as Sophie took in the magnificent foyer that extended up to the second floor. Straight ahead was a fountain with a curved staircase flanking either side.

The chandelier's beaming lights bounced off the marble floor, the fresh floral arrangements at the base of each staircase were perfectly placed in large marble urns. Not only was the entrance something from a royal magazine but the fragrant aroma from the wintery mix smelled so inviting.

This setting could have easily been ripped out of a fairy tale and Roslyn wished more than anything she could let herself get swept away into this fantasy life.

"There's my city boy."

Sophie turned her attention to a tall striking woman with a stylish pixie cut. The silver-haired lady had on a pair of jeans and a bright green sweater paired with little silver sneakers. Not at all the image Sophie had had in her mind of the

Dame. But her relaxed style did put Sophie a little more at ease.

Nigel's grandmother came up and wrapped her arms around him before easing back and turning her focus, and affection, to Sophie. She found herself enveloped in a strong embrace and caught Nigel's smirk and smile over the shoulder of Dame Claire.

"Welcome, welcome," she greeted, pulling away from Sophie. "I'm Claire."

"It's a pleasure to meet you, Dame Worthington. I'm Roslyn Andrews."

Nigel's grandmother waved a hand and shook her head. "None of this Dame nonsense. Those titles are so archaic. Call me Claire. And while you're at it, tell me how you managed to capture my workaholic grandson's attention to get him to bring you here."

"Can we at least take our coats off and get settled before you start grilling her?" Nigel asked. "And you ordered me to bring a date, so don't pretend to be surprised."

"As if you ever listen to me," Claire muttered. "You've never brought a woman here in your life, so I'm already impressed with this one."

Sophie removed her coat and handed it to a man who seemed to appear out of nowhere, along with two others, to take their things.

Nigel had never brought a lady home? That was rather interesting. Did he mean it when he said he just wanted her here as a guise or did he actually want to spend alone time with her and have her meet his family?

Sophie didn't know what all the answers were and she couldn't wrap her mind around it now. If there was a chance that Nigel had truly wanted to share more of his life with her, then she feared the guilt would consume her. She wished she could go back and tell him everything, wished she could start fresh. Maybe then what they shared could actually be real.

But she couldn't go back and she definitely couldn't tell him the truth now.

"William said you had bourbon," Nigel said after the staff took their things.

"Your favorite," Claire replied with a wink.

"Oh, please. You introduced me to that brand when I turned eighteen and told me not to settle for anything less."

Claire laughed. "Guilty. So come on in and let's chat."

She wedged herself between Nigel and Sophie, looping her arms between them, and led them into another massive room with high ceilings. The fireplace on the far wall crackled with a warm fire and a tray of fruit, cheese, cookies, and other finger foods was set out on the table between the large leather sofas.

"Is Ellen here?" Nigel asked.

"She'll be along later. Your sister is very eager to see who you brought home."

Sophie settled onto the sofa next to Nigel and across from Claire. She hadn't realized she'd be this nervous to meet his family, but after their romp on the plane, she was a bundle of mixed emotions.

"Now, tell me how you met," Claire said, clasping her hands like a proud grandmother.

"At the office," Nigel piped in. "You know I have a policy about not dating employees, but Roselyn changed all of that."

They'd discussed their story and decided to keep it as close to the truth as possible.

Claire's eyes darted between them, then landed back on Nigel. "Do you always work? Wait, don't answer that. I know you do. Do you at least take this poor girl out to dinner?"

"Of course," Nigel replied, reaching for a lemon square. "We've had several work dinners."

"Nigel Phillip Townshend," she scolded.

He laughed. "I'm kidding. Relax."

Claire turned her focus to Sophie. "You must be a saint to put up with him. He's given me every one of my gray hairs, I tell you."

Sophie settled her hand on Nigel's knee. "Ignore him. One of the first things he asked when I started working with him was what my favorite food was."

"For work meetings?" Claire asked, raising one perfectly shaped brow.

"For a real date," Nigel chimed in. "I knew the second I saw her I wanted her as more than my consultant."

"Office romance. Well, it's your company and I think it's romantic…so long as you keep romance in the relationship and not just in the form of a spreadsheet."

"I like her," Sophie laughed, glancing to Nigel. "You had me afraid to come."

Nigel cringed and Claire let out a burst of laughter. "Did he, now? I'd love to hear what picture he painted of me."

"I'd like to know what he said about me, too."

Sophie turned to the entrance of the living area as a beautiful, curvy woman came striding through. Her long dark hair fell in waves over her shoulders and she looked as if she'd just come in from riding a horse given her tight black pants, tall brown boots, and bright red fitted jacket.

"Ellen, you're just in time." Claire came to her feet and kissed the woman who had to be her granddaughter on the cheek. "Nigel's girlfriend was just dishing on workplace romance and what he truly thinks of his family."

Nigel muttered a curse under his breath and rose to greet his sister. Sophie stood as well, nervous at encountering another family member. Maybe she could knock these little meetings out one by one and not be so nervous come the day of the wedding.

"Workplace romance?" she asked, eyeing Nigel. "Well, aren't you all candy hearts and bouquets of flowers."

"Actually, Roslyn doesn't like bouquets," he said. "She thinks they're clichéd."

She turned to him. "You remembered that?"

His eyes shifted from her eyes to her mouth and back. "I remember everything you've ever said to me."

Sophie's heart picked up and she knew then, Nigel wasn't faking a relationship. He meant what he'd said. And she knew in that moment he was getting in just as deep as she was... But did he know? Was he aware of how he looked at her with his emotions in his eyes?

Dread filled her stomach at the thought of Nigel getting hurt in the end. She had never wanted to crush anybody except Miranda. All she'd wanted to do was come to New York, scope out some cutting room floor footage and talk to some crew members. She'd wanted to be in and out in a week's time.

Yet here she was, spending the next five days in England pretending to be Nigel Townshend's girlfriend when she really wanted to be his everything in real life.

"Wait a minute," Ellen said, staring at Sophie. "You look familiar. I think I know you from somewhere."

Sophie froze as Ellen's brows drew in and she

pursed her lips in thought. Sophie had not come this far to be outed, but her disguise wasn't foolproof and Ellen was smiling like she might just know Sophie's dirty little secret.

Twelve

With Nigel out of the country, Lulu was set on getting Fee to agree to the spin-off—or at least the wedding episode for *Secret Lives*.

"If that's really what you want to do, I'll stand behind you," Lulu told Fee.

The cameras moved around but Lulu ignored them. She'd gotten more than used to having her entire life filmed. Today she was having lunch with Seraphina as they chatted about Fee's upcoming move to Texas. While she hated losing her best friend, she understood how much Fee loved Royal and the people there—not just Clint, though the love Fee had for her fiancé was certainly something special.

When the cast and crew had been there for Christmas at Miranda's estate, they'd all fallen a little in love with the charming town. And after those devastating fires, Lulu more than understood Fee's need to be with the man she loved in his hometown.

After all, hadn't they all wanted to land a cowboy?

Unfortunately, the only one who'd caught her eye, and gotten on her last nerve the entire time she was there, was Kace the snarky lawyer... The snarky lawyer who'd shown up at her penthouse just to talk a few days earlier. Sure, like they'd ever *just talked*. At this point, they couldn't be alone for two minutes without clothes falling off. Mercy, the things that man could do with his hands.

"Everything okay?" Fee asked, reaching for her water glass.

"What? Oh, yes. Sorry." Lulu smiled and pushed thoughts of Kace aside. "Just thinking."

"About anyone I know?"

Fee's eyes twinkled, her smile all-knowing. Lulu didn't keep secrets from her best friend, but she wasn't about to voice anything about Kace on camera. Sure, her admission to her attraction to the sexy Southern attorney would get ratings going, but she wasn't ready to share her feelings with the world or Kace. There had been enough footage of the two of them bickering during the cleanup from the fires last month. By the time this show aired that they were filming today, who knows where she'd stand with him. Would she tell him her feelings? Would he admit to his?

"Let's concentrate on you and your new love," Lulu stated, giving her friend a wink. "I say we throw a big going away party. I'll host and we'll do it on my rooftop terrace."

Fee lifted her glass in a mock toast. "You know I'm always up for a party."

"Perfect. I'll get everything together."

And playing the dutiful hostess would give her the distraction she needed from one Kace LeBlanc.

Lulu waited until the cameras left to pull out her begging for the wedding episode and questioning her friend about the spin-off. She loved Fee and didn't want to put her on the spot for all viewers to see.

Fingers crossed Fee would be in agreement for both. Nigel was counting on Lulu to make all of this work out and she didn't want to let him down.

"That was weird how my sister insisted she'd seen you before," Nigel stated, gesturing for Sophie to enter their second-floor suite.

Sophie's heart still hadn't gone back to a regular rhythm after that close call. The scrutiny with which Ellen kept staring had had Sophie ready to hop back on Nigel's jet and head back to New York.

"Weird," she agreed, for lack of anything else to say.

As she eased past him and into the room, Sophie gasped at the view. A wall of patio doors leading out onto a private balcony drew her across the room, ready to take in the beauty of the land from above.

Heavy gold drapes outlined each side of the doors and she was positive no royal palace was arranged more beautifully. Her decorator eye would take in all the details of the room later, but she wanted to step onto the balcony and look over the snow-covered grounds.

"It's freezing out there," Nigel said when she unlatched one of the locks.

"I just have to see it for a moment. I'm imagining the beauty in the summer."

She shoved open one door and took in the crisp fresh air. Sophie blinked against the bright white covering of snow that stretched over the grounds for as far as her eye could see. The evergreens were accented with winter and she hated that she'd missed seeing this place all decked out for the holidays. She imagined perfectly decorated Christmas trees with gold-and-white stockings hung from each of the fireplaces, dinner parties with glamorous dresses, and champagne fountains.

She turned from the view and came back in, latching the lock behind her.

"You grew up here?" she asked.

"I lived here my entire life, except for my schooling, until I moved to New York." Nigel shoved his hands in his pockets and glanced around. "This is actually my room, not a guest suite."

Of course, they would be staying in his childhood room. If that didn't add another layer of guilt, nothing would. She wanted to come clean with him; she wanted to tell him everything. But how could she and still stay loyal to her brothers?

It was supposed to be so simple. A few days at Green Room Media, snooping for exclusive footage, chatting with some camera guys. In theory it all sounded like a perfect plot...but somehow the execution had gone astray and now she risked breaking her heart and hurting the one man who made her want to forget this entire vendetta.

"Quite the little prince," she joked. "Though I imagine you stood on your balcony and had the best imagination as a child. I know I would."

He smiled and started to cross to her. "And what would young Roslyn have imagined?"

Young *Sophie* would have loved this room. "She would have pretended to be a queen overlooking her land, protecting her castle and her family."

Not so far removed from grown-up Sophie.

"Really?" He closed the gap between them and took her shoulders in his hands. "That little girl wouldn't have dreamed of a knight coming to rescue her from the tower?"

"I've never needed to be rescued," she countered. "I'm the one who would save the day. Always."

Wasn't that what she was ultimately doing now? Sacrificing to save her family's legacy?

And who knew what would happen now that Darius was coming to Royal and Miranda wanted to connect with him.

One thing Sophie knew, she refused to let Blackwood properties, holdings and finances stay in the hands of a gold-digging socialite who probably already had her sights set on another unsuspecting wealthy man. Sophie couldn't figure out why she hadn't already remarried, but maybe the perfect billionaire hadn't come along, yet.

"You're very protective of your family," he stated, sliding his thumbs up along her neck and jawline. "I admire that."

He had no idea the lengths she'd go to.

"You and your sister must have a special bond," she replied. His touch had her body tingling and trying to concentrate on the actual conversation was difficult. "Since you are part of the wedding."

"We've always been close. She's older than me, so my grandmother doubled the pressure on her to settle down and have children." Nigel laughed. "Now that she's closing in on that goal, Grandmother has turned her attention solely on me. You've been warned."

Sophie reached up and gripped his wrists, returning his grin. "I can handle myself for a few days. Besides, I don't mind playing your girlfriend. You're not exactly an ogre."

Nigel's low laugh curled those nerves tighter in her belly. "I'll take that as a compliment. You're pretty sexy, too."

After the way he'd worshiped her body on the flight over here, she didn't need the words. She was well aware of how he thought of her. During their time on the jet, Sophie had pushed aside all of the outside problems facing them, all of the lies and deceit. She'd focused on them, on the pleasure and desire.

But reality hit hard now that they were here and she had to maintain the facade. Sophie only hoped she could get through these five days without Ellen circling back to how Sophie looked familiar.

"You know, we don't have to be down for dinner for a while," Nigel said, backing Sophie toward the four-poster bed.

"If we lose track of time and miss dinner, your grandmother will reprimand both of us."

Nigel shook his head. "If she thinks there's a chance you're going to help with the next genera-tion of Townshends, she'll lock us in here and to hell with all dinners."

The idea held its temptations...but she knew it was nothing more than a fantasy. Even without the deception hanging between them, Sophie was sure this world wasn't for her. The Townshends were pretty much as powerful and wealthy as royalty. And even though the Blackwoods were wealthy in their own right, the differences were vast. City and country life were quite different. Nigel may have grown up in this gorgeous countryside town, but he was all city. He was larger than life, someone who needed that hustle and hard work. Royal, Texas, wasn't for someone who needed that rush of moving from one project to the next.

Sophie, on the other hand, loved her laidback lifestyle back home. She loved the ease of her work, the thrill of designing for others at her own pace.

Nigel kissed her neck and Sophie realized how silly and foolish she was being by thinking there would ever be anything more between them. Instead of a foundation for a true relationship, they had a fling, they had a farce for the next few days, and they had her lies. Not exactly future-building material.

"I thought we were faking this relationship," she murmured, thrusting her fingers through his hair.

"Only some parts." His lips moved over her heated skin. "I want you. Nothing about that is a sham."

She couldn't argue, not when she wanted him just as fiercely.

In a flurry of hands and stolen kisses, their clothes fell to the floor. Sophie stumbled back onto the bed and Nigel followed her down, pressing his weight against hers and into the soft thick pile of blankets.

Sophie hadn't known she had such passion inside her until she met Nigel. Never before had she wanted to forget her goals and give everything, including and especially her body, to one man.

"I'll be right back."

Nigel eased off the bed, leaving her to watch as he crossed the room. The brightness from the daylight filtered in through the glass doors, casting a glorious glow on his magnificent form.

She didn't even try to turn away or hide the fact she was blatantly staring.

Nigel rummaged around through his luggage until he pulled out a box of condoms. Sophie laughed.

"Wow. Feeling optimistic, aren't we?"

He shrugged. "Hopeful. Besides, we're here for five days."

"Are you planning on us leaving this room?" she asked as he stalked back toward her. "You do have a wedding to be in."

"Oh, I wouldn't miss my sister's wedding." He sat the box on the side table and climbed back on the bed. "I also wouldn't miss the chance to explore this body again. I don't think I appreciated it enough on the plane."

"Oh, I'd say you appreciated me more than enough," she laughed. "Maybe it's my turn."

With a bold confidence she'd never felt before, Sophie came up to her knees and pressed her hands on his bare chest. She shoved him back onto the bed and straddled his lap.

"I think you've had enough control for once."

Leaning back against the headboard, Nigel placed his hands behind his head and smiled. "I'm not about to argue with a beautiful woman."

She had no idea what she was doing. She only knew she wanted total power over him for this moment, so she let her desires guide her.

Sophie reached across to the nightstand and grabbed a condom. There was no hiding her shaking hands as she tore open the wrapper and carefully covered him.

He never took his eyes off her.

That intense stare added to her nerves…and her arousal. This man could be so potent without saying a word or even reaching for her. The way he looked at her, like she was the most important thing in his life, was so foreign to her. She could tell he was falling for her, even if he hadn't said so or maybe he didn't even realize it himself.

But she couldn't, wouldn't, dwell on emotions right now. Nigel had awakened something inside her and she wanted to spend their time together not worrying about the issues back home. For the duration of her stay here, she would play the dutiful girlfriend and sultry lover.

Those would be the easiest lies she'd ever told.

Bracing her hands on his chest, Sophie joined their bodies. The moment they connected, she let out a sharp cry. This was so much different than what she'd experienced earlier. She didn't know if it came from the dominance on her part or the position, but Sophie closed her eyes as sensation after glorious sensation rolled through her.

Nigel's hands gripped her hips and she lifted her eyes to focus on him. Yeah, there was that look, the one she could identify—something stronger than lust...something she feared would get them both hurt.

Ignoring the impending broken heart, Sophie placed her hands on either side of his head and leaned down. Her hair curtained them both as she slid her mouth over his. She wanted everything he had to offer and more. She wanted to consume him, to join with him in every way. The ache in her body grew as her hips pumped against his. The spiral of euphoria slithered through her as she tore her lips away and cried out.

Nigel gripped her backside as his own body jerked and trembled. Sophie watched as the pleasure overcame him, and she wondered if anything could ever compare to this moment.

She didn't believe so. All she could do was enjoy

these next few days, because when they got back to New York, she was going to have to finish her plan and head home as soon as possible. The longer she spent with Nigel, the more she worried he might just be the one she hadn't known she was looking for.

Thirteen

Nigel didn't know why he was so damn nervous, but he stood outside of his suite door and adjusted his bowtie. He hated these bloody things, but since he had to stand up with the groom, he had to wear one.

He'd left Roslyn to get ready on her own while he'd gone to see if anyone needed help with setting things up for the ceremony. Ellen had decided to get married in the grand ballroom of the estate and there were bustles of wedding planners, florists, caterers, and who knows who else all around the east wing on the main level.

Nigel had ended up in the study, reading texts

from Seraphina telling him she was so sorry, but she and Clint had made the decision not to film a spin-off. She went on and on about how she knew this would not be what Nigel wanted—assuring him that she'd had a lengthy conversation with Lulu about the prospect of a new show—but Fee wanted to let him know that she was certain it wasn't for her. She would be happy to talk contract removal once he returned home.

Nigel cocked his head from side to side, try-ing to alleviate some of the pressure of this bloody buttoned-up shirt and tie. He had no clue what to do about Fee's contract right now, and that was something he'd have to put on the back burner—at least for today.

His sister was getting married and Roslyn was no doubt going to looking breathtaking. He'd had five gowns for her to choose from that his personal stylist had assured him any woman would love.

He tapped his knuckles on the door and then reached for the knob. The moment he pushed it open, every thought vanished as he took in the sight of Roslyn across the room, standing in front of the floor-length mirror.

Her eyes met his in the reflection as she fastened one earring. Her honey blond hair fell in waves over one shoulder and the ruby red strapless gown fit as if the designer had all of those luscious curves in mind.

The material draped down in the back and scooped low in the front. A little flare at the bottom only accentuated Roslyn's pinup shape.

"I hope you like it," she told him, turning to face him and smoothed her hands down the front of the dress. "I know it's a little flashy for a wedding, but someone told me red was your favorite color."

Flashy? More like elegance and sex all rolled into one. The dress, the woman… It was all utterly perfect.

Nigel moved on into the room and smiled. "You've been talking to my grandmother."

"Maybe."

Nigel stopped before he reached her, afraid if he got too close they may never leave this room. The sight of her had him forgetting any issues with *Secret Lives* and the dealings back in New York.

"I don't think it's customary to show up the bride," he told her.

"Oh, I doubt I could do that," Roslyn laughed. "I haven't seen Ellen's wedding dress yet, but I'm certain she's going to be stunning."

"I'm positive I won't be able to take my eyes off you. Maybe we could skip the ceremony and just hit the reception."

When he started to reach for her, she skirted around him with another laugh.

"You're a groomsman," she reminded him. "I'm

pretty sure your family would notice if you weren't there."

"With the way you look right now, I don't really care what my family thinks." He took a step toward her, his gaze raking over her once more before landing on her eyes. "I couldn't imagine being here without you."

Roslyn's smile faltered and she glanced down to her hands.

Nigel reached for her, curling his hands around her arms. "Everything alright?"

Her dark eyes came back up to his. "I need to tell you something."

Good conversations never came from that starting point. Nigel smoothed his thumbs across her skin, toying with the thin straps across her arms.

"You look worried," he told her. "Whatever it is, you can tell me. I trust you."

She opened her mouth, then closed it. A moment later she pasted on a smile that he knew she'd forced.

"I just…"

Worry rolled off her in waves so Nigel leaned forward and slid his lips over hers for a second before easing back.

Roslyn licked her lips and sighed. "I think I'm falling for you."

Well, that wasn't what he'd thought she would say and he had to admit, he wasn't surprised. Scared like hell that the words were out in the open, but not actually surprised. He wasn't oblivious to how she looked at him, how she touched him.

"I know it's wrong," she went on in a hurry. "We're supposed to be faking this while we're here, but—"

"Roslyn." He had to stop her. "You're intriguing, you challenge me, you're sexy as hell and I enjoy our time together. I just... I can't offer love. I'm married to this show, to growing it even bigger. A relationship with love and commitment... I don't know when I could offer that. You deserve more than I'd be able to give you."

Roslyn closed her eyes and shook her head. "I should've kept my feelings to myself," she muttered.

"No," he countered. "I'm glad you shared what you're feeling. I just...can't say the same. I care for you, but love isn't something I can do."

She returned her anxious gaze to his, but Nigel kissed her forehead. He wished he could give her everything she deserved, everything she wanted. But love was huge and he couldn't commit to something so strong, so permanent right now...not when he was in limbo of making or breaking the show he'd worked so hard to produce.

"Besides, there's plenty about me you don't know," he retorted. "Let's enjoy the day and then we can work on taking things slow once we get back to New York."

"I don't think New York and slow belong in the same sentence," she stated. "But, I agree. We should enjoy today and then we'll talk later."

Nigel wrapped her in his arms and wondered if she was the one. His grandmother had already fallen in love with Roslyn, but Nigel wondered if all of this was too good to be true.

Were they meant to be? He'd known her such a short time, but he couldn't ignore the strong pull or the deep connection they'd already formed.

But he also had to remember that the show came first for now. There was too much going on, too many people depending on him and his social life; his *love* life would not be taking top priority.

Sophie swayed in Nigel's arms in the ballroom. Try as she might, she couldn't forget the overwhelming guilt she'd felt when he'd told her he wanted to get to know her more. She'd opened her mouth and her thoughts, her feelings had come tumbling out and she couldn't take them back.

She'd wanted to come clean about everything. She hated lying to this amazing man, but instead of telling him the full truth about her background, she'd told him her honest feelings instead.

How could she love him, though? How could she make such a claim when he didn't even call her by her own name?

She'd taken something so beautiful, so mind-blowing, and turned it into something ugly and fake. What would he say when he found out why she'd infiltrated his company to spy on a woman he likely considered a friend?

Sophie gripped his shoulders and closed her eyes as the soft music enveloped them on the dance floor. He would no doubt hate her once he discovered who she truly was and she deserved nothing less.

But she would relish this fantasy moment for as long as she could. She didn't want to ruin his sister's wedding. But once it was over, she was going to have to tell him. If he wanted to get to know her more, if there was even an inkling of a chance for them, he'd need to know the truth before things went any further.

First, she'd have to talk to her brothers because all of this started when she'd vowed to find dirt on Miranda. There was overwhelming evidence that nothing sinister existed on the woman. Maybe she wasn't a monster like they thought. It was a possibility they had to consider, but then what would they do? Sophie still wanted the childhood home and estate to go back to her brothers. The home had to stay in their family…it just had to. But if they couldn't challenge Miranda in court, what other option did they have?

She would have to figure out what the next move should be once she spoke with Vaughn and Kellan.

Miranda aside, Sophie couldn't lie to Nigel anymore. Her feelings far surpassed anything she'd expected and now that she was in so far, she couldn't keep deceiving him. Once he discovered who she was, Sophie would just have to accept any backlash she received.

The song came to an end and Sophie pulled back. "I'm going to grab a glass of champagne."

Nigel drew his brows together. "Everything okay? You seem like you're not all here."

She hadn't been *all here* since she'd started this whole charade, but she nodded.

"Why don't you dance with your grandmother while I take a breather?"

He stared another moment before nodding and releasing her. Sophie gathered the skirt of her dress in one hand and maneuvered her way off the dance floor. Somewhere in the back of her mind, she'd logged the beauty of the reception with all the lighting and crystal beading draped from the elegant table arrangements and the chandeliers suspended from the high ceilings, casting a kaleidoscope of colors across the marble floor.

There were gorgeous people everywhere dressed in stunning gowns and sharp suits. And Sophie felt like such an imposter…likely because she *was* an imposter.

She'd barely stepped away from the dancers when a member of the wait staff came by with a tray of champagne glasses. Sophie smiled and grabbed one, needing something to hold to occupy her shaky hands.

"Thank you for coming."

Sophie spun around to see Ellen smiling and holding her own glass.

"Of course," Sophie replied. "You had the most beautiful wedding I've ever seen."

Her satin gown was positively radiant, showcasing a vintage vibe with a lace overlay. It was strapless with a flare from the waist and a delicate train. Her headpiece was a simple diamond headband with a sheer veil that trailed the length of her train. Three strands of crisp white pearls adorned her neck.

"I mean, thank you for coming home with my brother," Ellen clarified. "I've never seen him this happy and I'm pretty sure I have you to thank."

"Oh, well, he makes me pretty happy, too."

"You're good for him," Ellen said, then took a sip of her champagne. "I hope he'll come home more often—and bring you with him. I've always wondered what it would be like to have a sister."

"I have two brothers, so I know how that feels," Sophie replied with a laugh.

But the guilt continued to mount. Her lies had trickled so far off course from the simple plan she'd initially concocted. Now she was lying to sweet, innocent people, intruding in this family event where she didn't belong. She'd likely be in photographs of this day and when Nigel or Ellen saw them, they'd have to relive this all over again. The betrayal and the deceit.

Ellen reached for her hand. "Then I do hope we can get to know each other more. I swear I feel like I know you from somewhere, but it must just be how quickly we connected. You know how with some people, you just have that instant click."

Yeah, that must be it.

"Anyway, I'm just really glad my brother found someone he actually wanted to bring home," Ellen went on. "He's always so busy working, maybe you can convince him to take more time off and visit his family."

"I'll see what I can do," Sophie promised with a smile.

Ellen leaned in and gave a one-armed hug before turning back to the reception and her guests… leaving Sophie alone with her drink and thoughts bouncing around. Even though this was all based on lies, Sophie had very good intentions, but she didn't know if anyone other than her brothers would see that.

Even a glass of champagne wasn't making Sophie feel better or helping her forget her problems. Once this magical day was over and she and Nigel were on their way back to New York, she would have to talk to him. She might have started this whole vendetta against Miranda, but the entire plan had snowballed and what could have potentially been the greatest thing in Sophie's life was now likely ruined to the point of no return.

Nigel swirled his grandmother around on the dance floor and caught Sophie's eye. When he sent her a wink, her entire body jolted from love.

She did love him. There was no denying the truth now that it stared her in the face…literally.

Now she had to figure out if she could clean up this mess she'd created, manage to reclaim her rightful inheritance, and hold on to the man she didn't know she'd been looking for. Oh, and wait to see if he could fall for her because he was still unsure.

Sophie didn't see a way to get out of the impending broken heart and she had nobody to blame but herself.

Fourteen

Sophie bundled her coat closer around her neck as she made her way from the car to Nigel's jet. They'd spent another day at Shrewsbury Hall after the wedding, but now they needed to get back to work.

And she needed to get back to reality...which meant she needed to tell Nigel the truth.

Sophie figured once they were settled in for their flight would be the perfect time. He couldn't storm out and maybe she could get him to see how all of this had gotten out of her control.

Not that she would make excuses. There were none. She'd blatantly lied to him and each time he called her Roslyn, she felt…well, like she was her own dirty little secret.

How could she have expected to prove Miranda was evil when Sophie had been doing evil herself?

Sophie boarded the jet as nerves curled through her. She'd spoken with both of her brothers last night and they supported her decision to tell Nigel. They'd agreed that maybe there was no dirt to be found on Miranda. They would have to find another way to get their property.

Settling into one of the white leather sofas, Sophie fastened her seat belt as she waited for Nigel to finish speaking with the pilot. She wasn't nearly as nervous about flying this time, perhaps because she had too much on her mind. No matter how many times she rehearsed her speech, she was terrified to just let those words out in the open.

Nigel stepped through to the cabin and his eyes immediately locked with hers. Her time was up.

"Are we all set to go?" she asked.

Nigel sighed and settled back against his seat. "We're all good."

"You don't sound good."

He lifted a shoulder and glanced back at her as he laced his fingers in hers. "I hate leaving my family. It never gets easier. That's the real reason I don't visit more. My grandmother thinks it's because I work so much, but that's not it. I can carve out time, it's just difficult to come here and then have to leave again."

Sophie understood that need to be close to family. She loved her brothers with her entire heart and couldn't imagine living in another country where she couldn't see them anytime she wanted.

"Do you ever think of moving back?" she asked.

"Not really," he admitted. "I mean, I love it here, but I've made a home and a life in New York. I need to visit home more often, though."

"Your grandmother and sister would love that," Sophie told him. "Family means everything at the end of the day."

"I agree. Which is why I'm hoping you'll join me when I return next month."

"What?"

Sophie stilled. Return with him? He couldn't mean that. He couldn't really want her to come back. First of all, this was just pretend and second of all, in a month, they likely wouldn't be speaking.

Her heart hurt because he stared at her with such hope in his eyes while he waited on her answer.

"My family seemed to take you in as one of their own and if we're getting to know each other more and more, it only seems right that you come back with me." He shrugged. "I mean, if you want to."

Roslyn closed her eyes just as the plane took off down the runway. Her breath caught in her throat but the fear she had of flying took a backseat to the fear she had of breaking Nigel's heart.

She simply couldn't do it. Not now. Not when he was pouring out his raw, honest feelings. He may not have been using the *L* word, but he was already inviting her back and that spoke volumes.

He literally was handing her everything, and if she told him the truth now, she would be throwing it all right back in his face. He would hate her.

There had to be a better way.

"I've got you," he murmured, squeezing her hand when the plane tipped up. "Just breathe."

He thought she was being silent and avoiding speaking to him because of her fear… If only he knew.

If only he knew her real name, her story…would he still want anything to do with her?

Sophie opened her eyes and shifted to face him. "I'd love to come back with you, but first I want you to meet my family. Well, my brothers. Then we'll see if you still want me to join you."

Nigel's smile widened. "You think I'm going to meet your brothers and get scared off? Are they that bad?"

"They're wonderful." But the truth was brutal. "I just want you to know everything about me before we go any further."

He stared at her another minute and Sophie wished she could just get up the courage to tell him the truth right now like she'd mentally prepared herself to do, but she couldn't.

"I'd love to meet your brothers," Nigel told her as he leaned in and slid his hand across her cheek and through her hair. "I want to know everything about you, Roslyn Andrews."

Sophie Blackwood.

It was on the tip of her tongue, but she said nothing like the coward she was.

How could she ever accuse Miranda of anything at this point? Sophie had betrayed Nigel day after day and she'd had the nerve to call it love. But she did love him. She'd made a mistake that she couldn't take back and there was no way she could've ever seen this disaster coming. Never before in her life had she purposely set out to hurt someone, to blatantly lie to someone's face. Going into this whole charade, she knew she'd be lying, but she honestly didn't think the end result would be so painful for so many.

The guilt and shame settled heavy in her heart as Nigel kissed her. The intimacy poured out of him and she just hoped he could find it in his heart to forgive her.

"Do you have a second?"

Nigel turned from his office windows and faced the doorway where Miranda stood.

"For my biggest star? Of course."

Miranda laughed as she stepped in and closed the door at her back. "I know I can always count on you for an ego boost."

Nigel truly did love each of the *Secret Lives* ladies in different ways. Miranda was genuine and loving. Always eager to help others. He couldn't imagine anyone not feeling drawn to her, though he'd heard about her difficult relationship with her ex-stepchildren.

Nigel knew Miranda and the Blackwood siblings didn't get along, but he really never understood why. Then again, he didn't know the Blackwood kids, either.

He'd never had one problem with Miranda and he respected her as a businesswoman and an asset to his show.

"What are you doing in New York?" he asked. "If you'd told me you were coming, I would've arranged lunch."

"Oh, don't worry about that." Miranda tucked her red hair behind her ear. "I was in town for a few meetings with some potential investors for Goddess Inc."

Goddess Inc. was Miranda's baby, which happened to be the country's fastest growing fitness empire. The woman was a force and she had already made a huge impact in the industry.

"I can have dinner arranged for us," he told her. "I have a new consultant that I'd like to introduce you to. She's got some great ideas about the show and how to boost ratings."

"I'd love to meet her," Miranda stated.

Nigel shoved his hands in his pockets and leaned back against the window ledge. "So, what brought you by? I know you didn't just pop in to say hi."

Miranda adjusted the clutch beneath her arm and shook her head. "I'm worried about Fee. With her leaving the show and all."

Nigel pulled in a deep breath. "As much as none of us want to lose her, change can sometimes be a good thing."

"She told me you asked her to consider a spin-off."

"I did and she decided to just make a fresh start with her new life, without all of the cameras." Nigel shrugged. "I can't blame her. I don't like it and I want her to change her mind, but I can see why she'd want to just enjoy her new marriage without any added stress."

Miranda pursed her lips. "Are you looking to re-place her on the show?"

He'd thought about that. He actually wanted to discuss that with Roslyn, but since they'd gotten home from England yesterday, he'd been so busy playing catch up. Work that he hadn't been able to handle through emails and long-distance phone calls had become a bit of a pile, so he hadn't had the chance.

"I haven't decided on that just yet," he answered honestly. "We may see how things go without. I hope I can talk Seraphina into making a guest appearance every now and then."

At least they could work out the rest of her contract doing things that way.

"Let me set up dinner reservations and we can talk more," he told Miranda as he reached for the phone.

"Oh, no." Miranda waved a hand. "I actually have to get back to Texas. I have a few things still to clear up after Buck's death."

"Well, next time you're coming to town, you'd better give me a heads-up," he warned with a smile.

"Of course I will," she promised.

Miranda crossed the room and kissed his cheek. "I'll see if I can talk to Fee about those guest appearances. It might sound sincerer coming from a friend and not the man writing her checks and talking about contracts."

Nigel nodded. "I'd appreciate that."

Miranda left his office almost as quickly as she'd come. He really didn't know what to do about Fee leaving. A few weeks ago that news would've stressed him out and had him losing sleep. But since meeting Roslyn and having her occupy most of his thoughts, work wasn't as stressful.

Part of him felt like a teen with a crush. Which was absurd since he was well into his thirties. He didn't want Roslyn to be too good to be true. The fact she gave herself to him for the first time spoke volumes for her character and her feelings toward him. He knew she couldn't have been intimate with him had she not felt so strongly about him.

He was supposed to meet her brothers soon. Roslyn promised to have them come to New York and they'd all meet at her penthouse for dinner. He was excited to get to know all facets of her life, but he didn't know why she'd seemed so worried. Her family couldn't be complete monsters. Besides, he wanted to try to explore the idea of more with her. He'd told her he couldn't love her, he didn't have it to give, but that had been fear. He wouldn't have taken her home if he wasn't feeling something stronger for her.

Nigel wanted to see just how far this would go and there was nothing that would change his mind.

Fifteen

Sophie stepped from her office just as a flash of red hair caught her eye.

The gasp escaped her as she turned back into her office and quickly shut the door.

Miranda was here? Why? Did she know what Sophie was doing? Had she come to rat her out?

Sophie leaned back against the door, trying to listen, but she heard nothing. With her breath caught in her throat, Sophie closed her eyes and tried to remain calm. If Miranda had revealed her secret and Nigel knew the truth, he'd be in here any second.

Craig's muffled voice echoed down the hall followed by Miranda's laugh. Good, she was moving away from Sophie and Nigel's offices.

Just keep going. Get on that elevator and get the hell out of here.

Sophie had known there was a possibility Miranda might show up at the office, but considering Sophie had planned on getting in and out in a week, she hadn't been too worried.

Now, well, she'd been here a couple weeks and knew she was tempting fate with each additional day she stayed.

Sophie had texted her brothers and asked how soon they could get to New York. She'd told them everything and pleaded with them to help her with Nigel. Maybe that was still a coward's way out to have backup, but she was desperate to hold on to the best thing that had ever happened to her.

Hopefully Vaughn and Kellan could be here tomorrow and Sophie could get all of her lies out in the open and tell Nigel exactly who she was and why she'd deceived him. She had to make him understand that every part of what happened between them was real—especially the part where she was falling in love with him.

Until all of this mess was over, Sophie wasn't going to be able to relax. And now she had to watch out for more Miranda sightings. Perhaps she should stay in her office or, better yet, feign sickness and head to her penthouse where she could hide out until she could confront Nigel.

Either way, Sophie was walking a thin line and at any second she could fall off and get lost in her web of deceit.

Nigel had just eased into the back of his car when his cell rang. He'd spent twelve hours at the office today trying to formulate a game plan for some grand going away party for Seraphina. Of course, the event would be aired, but the show needed to be the grandest of all. A black-and-white cocktail party at the Waldorf? A luau in Hawaii? He wasn't sure what would be the best, but he did plan on getting Roslyn's take on several ideas.

As his driver pulled away from the curb, Nigel answered his phone without looking.

"Nigel Townshend."

"Always so professional."

He smiled at his sister's teasing tone. "Aren't you supposed to be on your honeymoon?"

"I'm in Morocco now," she told him. "We just arrived after a couple days in Spain. It was beautiful, by the way, thanks for asking."

Nigel laughed and settled into his seat. He dropped his head back and closed his eyes. He'd take even a second of relaxation at this point. Trying to figure out ways to save his show from plummeting into an abyss while losing one of their top cast members was quite stressful.

Which was just another reason he couldn't wait to see Roslyn. She always made things seem better, brighter.

"So why are you calling your brother when you should be spending time in newly wedded bliss?"

"Are you alone?" she asked.

"I just left the office, so I'm with my driver." Alarm bells went off in his head. "What's going on? Are you okay?"

"I'm fine, but I'm worried about you."

"Me? Why?"

Ellen sighed. "You remember how I kept saying Roslyn looked familiar to me?"

"I do."

"I don't know how to tell you this," she murmured.

Nigel sat up and gripped his cell. "Just say it," he demanded. That trickle of fear down his spine had him on edge.

"Her real name is Sophie Blackwood."

Blackwood. As in… Miranda's late ex?

"She's actually a famous designer," Ellen went on. "I was watching one of my favorite YouTube channels on the plane and that was when it hit me. She has a massive following on her channel *Dream It, Live It*. I've watched so many of her design videos that I should have recognized her right off the bat, but she's altered her look. She's not a blond naturally and she doesn't usually wear glasses."

Nigel rubbed his forehead as his sister's words settled in.

"Are you positive?" he asked, hoping she wasn't, but knowing she was or she never would've called.

"Yes. I'm sorry."

Nigel's chest constricted. His driver continued toward Roslyn's penthouse. No, *Sophie Blackwood's* penthouse.

Why the deception? Because of Miranda? To get back at her for some reason? He didn't know the answers, but he sure as hell deserved them...starting with why she had used him, going so far as to tell him she was falling in love with him.

Going so far as to sleep with him over and over.

Nigel clenched his jaw and willed himself to remain calm. He had to talk to Roslyn...or whatever the hell she wanted to call herself. He had to hear her side, though he couldn't imagine there was a defense strong enough to make him forget what she'd done or warrant forgiveness.

"Nigel," Ellen said. "Are you still there?"

"I'm here. I'm on my way to her penthouse right now."

"I'm sorry," she said again. "I don't want you hurt."

Hurt? Yeah, he was, but bloody furious might be closer to his current mood.

"Will you text or call me later?" she asked. "I'm worried about you."

"I'll be fine," he lied. "Thank you for telling me—you did the right thing. Go enjoy your honeymoon and we'll talk when you get back."

Nigel disconnected the call and immediately typed in *Dream It, Live It* in his phone's browser. His heart sank when a smiling brunette popped up onto the screen. She casually leaned against the side of a pale yellow sofa. She wore a pretty floral dress with very little makeup and she was actually barefoot and holding a glass of wine. She had her head tipped just so and a perfect smile for the camera.

This was his Roslyn.

No. This was Sophie Blackwood with millions of followers. She was clearly a major success—and not at all in need of a job. Yet, she'd come to Green Room Media and infiltrated herself as a consultant, going so far as to sleep with her boss…and for what? Obviously something to do with Miranda, but Nigel didn't know why he'd gotten involved in this family drama.

He clicked through the different thumbnail photos of the videos. She certainly did look different with all that rich dark hair.

Bloody hell. She looked sexier, more natural.

And he still got that tug of arousal when he saw that smile and those curves. No amount of betrayal could turn that off.

"Sir, should I wait?"

Nigel realized the car had come to a stop. He shoved his phone back into his pocket and reached for the handle.

"I'm not sure how long I'll be," he replied. "Just don't go too far."

"Yes, sir."

Nigel had no clue what would happen once he confronted Ms. Blackwood. Right now she felt like a total stranger. He'd told her he wanted to get to know her more on a deeper level, but he'd had no idea he didn't know her at all. He hadn't even known her damn name.

Everything over the past few weeks had been a lie and Nigel wasn't leaving here until he got the answers he deserved.

The guard had alerted Sophie to a visitor and Sophie granted him permission to come on up. She glanced around the penthouse and onto the balcony where she'd set up a late-night dinner. She knew Nigel had been working so hard.

She wanted to do something for him to let him know she admired the way he juggled everything. She also wanted to pamper him just a bit.

Vaughn and Kellan had reluctantly agreed to come tomorrow, so this would be the last night Sophie would have with Nigel before he discovered the truth. She just wanted one more magical evening with the man she loved before she potentially lost him forever.

A heavy lump of guilt settled in her throat. Time was running out and she would have to make the most of every moment tonight.

When the elevator chimed and slid open, she glanced across the penthouse as Nigel stepped out. He'd clearly been raking his hands through his hair. The stress of the show was getting to him. She offered a smile, but it dropped into a worried frown when he didn't return the gesture.

"Rough day?" she asked.

"You could say that."

Sophie crossed to the island bar and grabbed the drink she'd made for him.

"I thought you could start with a nice bourbon before dinner," she told him, handing him the tumbler of amber liquid. "I've set us up over next to the balcony so we can still see the beautiful view, but not freeze."

Nigel tipped back the drink and sat the glass back on the bar. He shoved his hands in his pockets, but remained silent. Work must have really kicked him down today. She'd never seen him so worn or quiet.

"I have good news," she told him. "I got in touch with my brothers and they can be here tomorrow. I'd love for us to all do a nice dinner if you think you can leave the office early enough."

She turned toward the island to start filling the plates with pasta.

"Your brothers," he repeated slowly. "Would that be Vaughn and Kellan Blackwood?"

The plate dropped from her grasp and shattered onto the floor.

"And that would make you Sophie," he added.

Sophie glanced over her shoulder. Nigel held up his phone to show her a muted video from her YouTube channel.

"I had no idea you were so popular until I discovered this," he went on. "Sophie Blackwood, a YouTube sensation and brilliant interior designer."

Sophie gripped the edge of the counter. "Give me a second to explain."

"A second? Oh, I think you'd need much longer than that, don't you? I mean, you've clearly been planning this for a long time." He dropped his arm and shoved the phone back into his pocket. "How long would you have gone on with this charade, *Roslyn*?"

Tears pricked her eyes, but she needed to put up a strong front and not be seen as weak. She needed him to understand her actions, her reasoning. He understood family loyalty, didn't he?

"That's why I wanted you to meet my brothers," she explained. "I wanted to tell you everything with them here so they could help me explain what we were up against."

Sophie started to step toward him, but glanced to the shards of the broken plate near her bare feet.

"You're going to cut yourself."

Nigel muttered a curse under his breath and stepped over the mess, the broken plate crunching beneath his shoes. He gripped her by the waist and lifted her up and over, setting her down safely a good distance away.

Even in his anger, he was still a gentleman. How could she not be in love with him? He obviously cared for her or her actions wouldn't have hurt him so much.

That sliver of information gave her hope. She knew he'd be hurt no matter how he discovered the truth, but she just wished she could've been the one to tell him. Now the betrayal seemed so much harsher.

"Who told you?" she asked.

Nigel shook his head. "That doesn't matter. You're the one who lied and used me."

Sophie recalled the flash of red yesterday.

"Miranda," she murmured.

"What?"

Sophie held his gaze. "Miranda told you, didn't she? I saw her at the office yesterday."

Nigel's eyes widened. "You saw her and didn't say anything? Afraid of getting caught?"

"I have valid reasons for everything I did."

The muscle in Nigel's jaw clenched and he

propped his hands on his hips. "Miranda didn't tell me anything, so clearly she doesn't know you're here."

In that case, Sophie had no idea how he found out, but it really didn't matter. All that mattered was that she'd hurt him. She had to find a way to make him understand why she'd done this. Would he believe her if she told him she'd give up the vendetta against Miranda for a second chance with him?

At this point, no. The shocking news was too fresh, the pain too raw.

"My father's will left everything to Miranda," Sophie started. "My brothers and I got nothing."

"So you're seeking revenge as some sort of poor little rich girl?"

Sophie swallowed and blinked back unshed tears. "I know that's what it looks like, but the money has nothing to do with it. Miranda doesn't deserve anything from my father. She just married him for the fortune—the ranch and all of its history mean nothing to her. She has my childhood home and everything else that should remain in the Blackwood family."

Nigel stared at her from the slit in his lids. "So you came here to what? Find dirt on Miranda and then blackmail her into giving you back what you want? That sounds petty and childish."

"No, it sounds like my brothers and I want our home back. We want to be able to keep that in the family," she cried. "Miranda doesn't care about Royal like we do. She has her own life, her own empire. My brother and his wife are expecting a child and we want to carry on the Blackwood legacy."

Sophie stared at him, waiting for some sign that he understood where she was coming from. That he might get her loyalty wasn't a bad thing even if she'd made a bad choice.

"And did you find what you were looking for?" he finally asked.

Sophie crossed her arms over her chest. "No. I didn't find anything negative on Miranda. And I certainly wasn't looking to fall in love."

Nigel let out a humorless laugh and turned from her. "Don't throw that word out, not now. You don't know what love is. You don't lie to the people you love and you sure as hell don't deceive them."

Sophie took a few steps forward, close enough that she could reach out and place her hand on his rigid back. He stiffened even more, but he didn't turn to face her.

"I never meant to deceive you," she stated. "When I applied for the job at Green Room Media, I wanted to talk to people, get some scoop against Miranda. I never ever thought I'd be working that closely with you."

"Yet you did." Now he did turn, causing her hand to fall away. "You got close to me. You slept with me and for all I know that was part of the plan."

He shook his head and raked both hands over his messy hair. "Once you realized you'd be working one-on-one with me, I'm sure that just fit right into your deceit. I mean, who better to get gossip from than the CEO? No one in the company has spent more time with Miranda than me. Giving your virginity was above and beyond, though."

"Stop," she ordered, the pain slicing her heart too deep. "I never wanted to be with a man until I met you. I knew in the end you'd find out who I was, but by the time I realized I loved you, it was too late for there to be any easy way to come clean. I was afraid of ruining things between us, so I didn't know how to tell you the truth. But you have to know that I couldn't have given myself to you had I not fallen so hard."

"All of this is so convenient," he mocked. "You just land a job with me, have access to nearly everything regarding the show and you get a free trip to Cumbria. I can't believe I was so naive not to trust my gut when I wondered if this was too good to be true."

"We don't have to be over," she said, her voice softening as the gnawing ache threatened to constrict her. "I know you're angry and confused and hurting. I also know I don't deserve to ask anything of you, but I'm asking that you take time and think before you just throw me out of your life."

"You think any of this is up to me?" he snarled.

"I'm not the one who threw this all away. You did. You could've told me at any point over the past weeks who you really were, but you opted not to. Or, hell, at the very least you could've told me when you claimed you started falling in love with me."

"Looking back, I see that," she admitted. "But that would have meant letting down my family— choosing you over the promise I made to them. I told my brothers I would follow through and find the information we needed. I didn't want to let them down."

Maybe appealing to the side of family loyalty would get _him_ to see she wasn't a complete monster.

"I'm the same person you were with in Cumbria," she told him. "I never lied to you about my feelings."

"You're not the same person at all," he countered. "I didn't even know your name."

Shame consumed her and she nodded. "But you know my touch and you know I love you. If you think back to our time together, you'll see that. You remembered what I said about that single stem, you know my food quirks, you know how well we mesh on a business level. We work together perfectly from every angle. Once you get beyond the shock and the anger, I hope you'll realize that no matter what happens, I'll always love you."

He said nothing, just continued to stare at her. Sophie wanted so badly to reach for him, to have him wrap his arms around her and tell her that he didn't hate her, that they would work this out.

But that was foolish thinking. His forgiveness was something she didn't deserve.

"I don't need to meet your brothers," Nigel finally said. "Needless to say, you're no longer welcome at Green Room Media and you're no longer part of my life. So go back to Texas and deal with your family drama there, but leave me out of it."

Without another word, he turned and headed to the elevator. Sophie watched as he stepped in and didn't even look back at her. She kept waiting, hoping for something else, but there was nothing. He'd literally cut her out just that fast.

The moment the doors slid closed behind him, Sophie let the tears fall. She'd brought all of this upon herself. There was nothing to show for her efforts—no dirt on Miranda and no relationship with Nigel. She was literally going back to Royal empty-handed, alone and in worse shape than when she'd arrived in New York.

Sophie turned toward the kitchen and stopped when she noticed the broken plate. Clearly the only thing she was good at lately was destroying everything around her. She only wished her heart would be as easy to clean up as this dish.

Sixteen

In the five days since he'd seen Sophie, Nigel still couldn't bring himself to go up to the penthouse of his own office building. The one space he'd always gone to for solace now held memories too painful to revisit.

He stared out the window of his office, watching the snow swirl around, remembering how the flakes would stick to Sophie's lashes.

Sophie. The name seemed to fit her, yet it was so strange to think of her that way. Like a bloody fool, he'd watched too many of her videos. Maybe he was just a masochist, but he'd wanted to see the real Sophie Blackwood in her element.

She'd positively shined and was so personable, so fun.

He hated to admit that he recognized in her the woman he'd started falling for. He'd thought Roslyn had been just a facade, but Sophie was the same, just like she'd said. And yet there was such a difference that he couldn't put his finger on. He tried yet again to push the thought away and refocus on work.

The gray skies didn't help his mood right now, neither did the fact that he couldn't pinpoint a location to have the farewell party for Seraphina. He wanted to make things as easy as possible for her and Clint.

His cell vibrated on his desk with an incoming text and Nigel glanced over his shoulder. Ellen's name popped up.

On a sigh, he grabbed his cell and opened the message.

I haven't heard much from you. I'm worried. Nana doesn't know anything because she just messaged me about "that nice American girl" coming back next month and doing a girls' luncheon.

Bloody hell. His grandmother would be heartbroken over all of this. Perhaps he should stick to the original plan of just telling her they broke up.

He didn't want to tell her that Roslyn was really Sophie and that she'd lied to them all.

Granted, he'd taken Sophie home under the pretense of her being his girlfriend so he'd lied, too.

This entire situation was a mess. So much deceit, so much pain.

Nigel typed back a quick text, telling his sister he was fine and just busy at work and that he'd take care of Nana.

He hadn't even put his phone down when it rang and Miranda's name appeared.

Nigel swiped the screen to answer.

"Miranda. What can I do for you?"

"I hope this isn't a bad time," she replied.

Considering he was wallowing in his own self-pity party, this was the perfect time for a distraction…unless there was more bad news.

"You're not leaving the show," he commanded.

Miranda's soft laughter came through the phone. "No, I'm not. I'm not calling about work. I'm calling about your personal life."

"Is that right?"

"Listen, I've never stepped foot into your private affairs, but I need to now," she went on. "I know Sophie was in New York trying to find something damning on me. I also know she was working for you."

Nigel crossed his office and sank down onto the leather sofa. "Did you know the entire time?"

"I found out before I left the office," she stated. "I pondered what to do with the information."

Nigel dropped his head back on the cushion and pulled in a breath. "So that's why you are calling me? She didn't find out anything, if that's what you're worried about. There's nothing negative about you to be found here, no matter how hard she looked."

"Well, I appreciate that, but that's not the reason for my call."

Nigel really didn't want to talk about Sophie to anyone. He'd even dodged talking to his own sister during these past several days.

There was no question he'd been falling in love with *Roslyn*, even though he'd tried to deny his feelings because he'd wanted to wait. The fact was, he'd been falling from day one. The pain wouldn't be so crippling and crushing if he'd just wanted her for sex. He missed her. He missed her smile, the way she'd hold his hand, her quick wit and sharp mind… He missed everything.

"I'm the last person who should come to her defense, but I am," Miranda went on. "Sophie and her brothers feel like they were wronged in the will after their father's death. I can't blame them for that. They've always thought I was after the Blackwood fortune. I wasn't, but given the way things happened with the will, their suspicious do make sense."

"Not to anyone who knows you," he informed her. "You don't have a callous bone in your body."

"Well, Buck left me strict orders before his death and I'm just trying to respect those wishes," she said. "Sophie is loyal to her family, Nigel. I truly believe she never meant to hurt you in any way."

Stunned, Nigel listened as Miranda defended her former stepdaughter. Nothing about that should have surprised him, though. Miranda was always the peacemaker, the one who would jump in to help anyone with no questions asked. She had a natural need to see those around her happy…even, apparently, those who were set on destroying her.

"I'm not sure why you'd want to help her out," Nigel said.

"Honestly, I'm helping you both," Miranda replied. "You know how gossip spreads. I learned that you took Sophie to England to Ellen's wedding. That tells me you really like her. I've never heard of you wanting to take someone home, let alone for a family wedding."

"It was a front to keep my grandmother off my back about settling down," he mumbled.

"That may be part of it," she agreed. "But don't discount your feelings. You don't have to tell me what they are. Just be honest with yourself. Enough lies were told and I wanted you to know the type of person Sophie really is. Her father wasn't the easiest man to love and he wasn't always the best to his kids, but he's trying to right a wrong from the grave and unfortunately, he's using me to do it—setting up enough of a mystery that the kids see me as an enemy."

Nigel had no clue what was all going on with that mess. But he knew Miranda's kind heart just wanted to make peace. He also knew she wouldn't have called if she didn't believe Sophie was a good person.

"You can do what you want, but I just had to share my thoughts," Miranda added. "And, if you were wondering, Sophie is going to be working on the Texas Cattleman's Clubhouse renovations. She's doing so free of charge and paying for the decor she uses. That information isn't public knowledge because she didn't want people to know. I believe that speaks to the type of woman she is."

Miranda said her goodbyes, leaving Nigel even more confused with his thoughts and his jumbled emotions. He had no clue what to do right now, and for the first time in his life, he felt utterly out of control.

All he knew was that he wanted this ache to cease. How the hell did he get over the one woman he wanted, but shouldn't?

Lulu smiled across the table at Kace.

"So, what do you say?" she asked, barely able to contain her excitement.

She'd asked Kace to lunch…not a date. This couldn't be a date. It just couldn't.

But the sexy cowboy attorney from Texas might just be the best add-in to *Secret Lives* if he'd simply agree to make a few guest appearances. When the show had filmed in Royal, the viewers had positively eaten up all the Southern charm those men had.

Of course there had only been one man who charmed Lulu enough to capture her attention and he sat right across from her still battling himself with the answer.

"Did you ask Nigel or the other women about this?" he finally asked.

Lulu picked up her water glass and took a drink. "I wanted to see what you said first. As for the other ladies, they'll totally be on board."

Who wouldn't? The man was a walking fantasy in a Stetson and shiny boots.

"Is this for the show's ratings or because you can't stand to be without me?" he asked with a smirk.

"The ratings, though I'm not sure we have it in the budget to pay you *and* your ego."

Kace eased back in his chair and propped one large strong-looking hand onto the table. Lulu couldn't ignore the desires just the sight of his hand pulled from her.

So what if her intentions to get him on the show

were because she wanted him around her more? She was human with basic needs. Maybe they'd been at each other's throats at one time, but sex changed everything.

"Just say you'll do it and leave the rest up to me," she urged. "Unless you hate the city life."

He let out a low sexy laugh. "New York isn't exactly my speed, but it's doable every now and then."

Lulu barely resisted the urge to leap over the table, straddle his lap and hug him. "Does that mean you'll do it?"

His kissable lips twitched. "If you can line up everything and get all the working parties to agree, I'll do it."

Lulu let out a slight squeal and clapped her hands together. "Perfect. You won't regret this."

Kace leaned across the table, taking her hands in his as he lowered his voice. "Make no mistake. You'll owe me."

And that sounded like the most delicious promise ever.

Seventeen

Sophie stared at her sketch pad and what she'd laid out so far, then she stared back at the nearly completed room. The architect and contractor had done a marvelous job of restoring the burnt portion of the clubhouse. Now she was trying to find a way to keep the decor true to the rest of the clubhouse, plus add in some special touches to really celebrate the reopening of this wing.

"Looks like some things still need decorated."

Sophie nearly dropped her sketch pad as she spun around at the familiar voice. "Nigel," she gasped. "What are you doing here?"

He casually leaned against the doorway that had

yet to be trimmed. With a gray T-shirt and worn jeans and even a pair of cowboy boots, he fit in perfectly. She'd never seen him in boots and she couldn't help but smile.

"Are you relocating to Texas?" she asked, nodding to his new attire.

With his hands in his pockets, he shrugged. "I figured I should at least try to look the part. I draw the line at the hat, though."

How could he have her smiling when looking at him hurt so much? But as conflicted as she felt, she knew he was here for a reason. She only hoped she was that reason.

"Did you come here looking for me or are you filming in Royal again?" she asked, unable to stand the anticipation.

"Maybe both," he replied.

Nigel pushed away from the door and took a slow walk around the open space. He didn't say a word as he continued to survey everything…which consisted of drywall, paint cans and etched glass windows.

Maybe he'd come to drive her crazy and make her pay for what she'd done to him. Although, she didn't know how much more she could suffer because living without him had been pure hell these past few days.

"I hear you're doing the decorating," he finally said as he focused his attention back to her.

Sophie clutched her pad to her chest. "I am. I wouldn't trust this to anyone else."

"I've seen your videos—you're good at what you do," he replied. "They're lucky to have such talent."

Stunned at his accolades, Sophie simply said, "Thanks."

Nigel took one step, then another, until he came to stand within inches of her. His eyes roamed over her face, her hair, before landing on her eyes.

"You dyed your hair back," he murmured, reaching out to smooth a strand behind her ear.

Sophie shivered at his touch and leaned in just enough to feel his warmth. "I wanted to get back to myself now that I'm home."

She didn't know how long they were going to do this small talk and dance around the proverbial elephant in the room. Seeing him again only reminded her of all that she'd had that she'd then thrown away...not that she'd thought of anything else since returning to Royal.

"I like this better," he told her as he dropped his hand, but didn't take a step back.

The familiar woodsy scent of his cologne enveloped her, making her recall laying against his chest and sleeping when they were in England. Making her remember when he'd first wrapped her in his jacket on that snowy night.

So many memories made in such a short time.

Nigel had packed such a powerful impact on her life and embedded himself so deeply into her heart.

"Why are you here?" she asked, unable to stand the silence and the nerves eating away at her.

"I'm here for you."

Fear ebbed away as hope flowed in. Sophie wanted to reach for him, but she needed to hear what he had to say. What had made him come all the way here instead of calling or texting? What happened in the five days after she'd left?

Because since she'd been back, all she'd thought of was where she could've righted her wrongs. But once she was caught in that downward spiral, she'd been completely out of control and she'd had no way to stop.

"I got a call from Miranda," he added.

Sophie blinked. "Miranda? What did she call you about?"

"You. She came to your defense without hesitation."

Seriously?

Sophie didn't know what to say to that remark. She'd never known Miranda to want to help her out. Of course, there was all those people who sang her praises and swore that Miranda was practically a saint, but Sophie hadn't experienced that side of her. Truth be told, they'd never really interacted much, not even when Miranda and Buck had still been married.

"What did she say?" Sophie asked.

Nigel smoothed a hand over his jaw and the back of his neck. He seemed so exhausted, which only matched her own situation. She hadn't slept for replaying the past few weeks over and over in her head. She wondered if he'd been awake all night thinking of her, too.

"She basically said that you had valid reasons for coming to New York."

How the hell had Miranda known Sophie was in New York? Had she seen her that day?

"I found out that Craig mentioned my new consultant when he was chatting with Miranda," Nigel went on. "I had actually talked to her about meeting you, obviously not knowing the truth, and then Craig was talking about how amazing you were and how you could be on the show because you're just as stunning as the others. I mean, you know how Craig gossips. He ended up showing Miranda a photo."

"She could've called me out right then," Sophie murmured. "Why didn't she?"

"I'd say she knew why you were there at that point," he told her. "But when she called me, she explained how you and your brothers feel cheated with the will and everything."

"We *were* cheated," Sophie reiterated. "We still don't understand why we were cut out."

"I get that." Nigel gave an understanding nod. "I don't get why you continued to lie to me, not once we started getting so close, but I know why you initially came to New York. You were trying to save your family's legacy. Believe me, I above anyone else understand the importance of showing family loyalty."

"I still don't understand why she came to my assistance," Sophie thought out loud.

Nigel reached for her arm and slid his fingers down to hold her hand. "Maybe because she's not the monster you all think she is. Maybe because she wants to see you happy. I truly believe she wants to fix her relationship with you and your brothers."

Sophie wasn't so sure about fixing things, but she also wasn't so sure that Miranda was out to take everything. She'd seemed just as surprised at the will as the rest of them. Maybe that hadn't all been an act.

"And her call made you come?" Sophie asked.

He squeezed her hand. "Her call made me think a little more about what this must have been like from your point of view. For years I've been somewhat of a black sheep for leaving England and not marrying or settling down. Family is important to me, even though I'm not jumping in to produce heirs."

Sophie smiled. After having met his grandmother and sister, and seeing where he came from, the archaic sounding trait wasn't so bizarre after all.

"Honestly, I couldn't stand being without you," he finally said. "The office was lonely, even though my staff is bustling all over the place. Every time I looked at events for the show coming up, I wondered what you would think or how you would change things. I can't even go up to my penthouse because I see you displayed on that couch. And now I can't go back to England because Nana thinks we're a couple."

Sophie smiled. "Is that all?"

Nigel took another step forward until they were toe-to-toe. He framed her face with his hands and leaned in, barely a breath from her mouth.

"No, that's not all," he whispered. "I love you and I want you. I won't ask you to give up your life here. I'd never do that. I'll fly back and forth if need be. I don't give a damn at this point, I just need you."

Sophie's heart nearly exploded. She never thought he would forgive her, and she sure as hell never thought Miranda would be the one to turn him around.

Had Sophie been wrong all this time? Was Miranda really just misunderstood and wanting to make things right?

Sophie wrapped her arms around Nigel's waist. "I need you, too. I've been miserable knowing that I hurt you. I just, I didn't know what to do and my loyalty was so torn—"

Nigel covered her lips, cutting off her sentence and any other thought she may have had. Nigel was here, he was holding her, kissing her and loving her. None of this was a dream and while she didn't deserve his forgiveness, she wasn't going to turn him away. She'd never take him for granted again.

Sophie eased back, sliding her fingers through his hair. "I swear, I'll never lie to you about anything ever again."

Nigel smiled. "That's good, but I hope you know what you're getting into with me."

"I have a pretty good idea."

"Maybe we'll need to make you an extra on the show," he stated. "I'm sure ratings would skyrocket with the most sought-after designer."

Sophie laughed. "Well, we'd have to marry and divorce since the show is about exes."

Nigel shook his head. "I'm never letting you go, but I'm sure I can sneak you in somehow."

He continued to stare at her and Sophie had never felt so excited and anxious and thrilled all at the same time.

"And you still have to come back home with me next month," he added. "My grandmother will grill you on babies and weddings."

Sophie met his gaze and grinned. "I'm open to both."

Nigel kissed her again, then wrapped his arms around her and picked her up, spinning her around.

"I'm never letting you go again," he told her. "I hope you don't mind a houseguest because I packed a large suitcase."

"Stay as long as you like," she told him.

"How about forever?"

Sophie kissed him again and knew she'd been given a second chance at her first love. Nothing could steal her happiness now.

* * * * *

Don't miss a single installment of
Texas Cattleman's Club: Inheritance

Tempting the Texan *by USA TODAY*
bestselling author Maureen Child

Rich, Rugged Rancher *by Joss Wood*
Available January 2020

From Boardroom to Bedroom *by USA TODAY*
bestselling author Jules Bennett
Available February 2020

Secret Heir Seduction *by Reese Ryan*
Available March 2020

Too Texan to Tame *by Janice Maynard*
Available April 2020

Her Texas Renegade *by USA TODAY*
bestselling author Joanne Rock
Available May 2020

Gage Striker vows to protect Mesa Falls Ranch from prying paparazzi at any cost—even when the press includes his former lover, Elena Rollins. Past misunderstandings fuel current tempers, but will this fire between them reignite their attraction?

Read on for a sneak peek of
Heartbreaker
by USA TODAY bestselling author Joanne Rock

Elena Rollins stepped toward him, swathed in strapless crimson silk and velvet. Her dark hair was half pinned up and half trailing down her back, a few glossy curls spilling over one bare shoulder. Even now, six years later, she took his breath away as fast as a punch to his chest. For a single devastating instant, he thought the smile curving her red lips was for him.

Then she opened her arms wide.

"April!" Elena greeted Weston Rivera's date warmly, wrapping her in a one-armed embrace like they were old friends.

Only then did Gage notice how Elena gripped her phone in her other hand, holding it out at arm's length to record everything. Was it a live video? Anger surged through him at the same time he wondered how in the hell she knew April Stephens.

"Were you unaware of Elena's day job?" Gage asked April as he plucked the device from Elena's red talons and dropped it in the pocket of his tuxedo jacket. "She's now a professional menace."

Elena rounded on him, pinning him with her dark eyes. They stood deadlocked in fuming silence. "That belongs to me," Elena sniped, tipping her chin at him. "You have no right to take it."

"You have no right to be here, but I see you didn't let that stop you from finagling your way onto the property."

She glared at him, dark eyes narrowing. "My video is probably still recording. Maybe you should return my phone before you cause a scene that will bring you bad press."

Extending a palm, she waited for him to hand it over.

"If you have a problem with me, why don't you tell it to the security team you tricked into admitting you tonight?" He pointed toward the door, where two bodyguards in gray suits were stationed on either side of the entrance. "You're trespassing."

"Is that a dare, Gage?" Her voice hit a husky note, no doubt carefully calibrated to distract a man.

It damn well wasn't going to work on him.

"I'm giving you a choice," he clarified, unwilling to give her the public showdown she so clearly wanted to record and share with her followers. "You can speak with me privately about whatever it is you're doing in my house, or you can let my team escort you off the premises right now. Either way, I can promise you there won't be any cameras involved."

"How positively boring." She gave him a tight smile and a theatrical sigh before folding her arms across her chest. "Maybe using cameras could spice things up a bit."

She gave him a once-over with her dark gaze.

He reminded himself that if she got under his skin, she won. But he couldn't deny a momentary impulse to kiss her senseless for trying to play him.

"What will it be, Elena?" he pressed, keeping his voice even. "Talk or walk?"

"Very well." She gestured with her hands, holding them up in a sign of surrender. "Spirit me away to your lair, Gage, and do with me what you will." She tipped her head to one side, a thoughtful expression stealing across her face. "Oh, wait a minute." She bit her lip and shook her head. "You don't indulge your bad-boy side anymore, do you? Your father saw to that a long time ago, paying off all the questionable influences to leave his precious heir alone."

The seductive, playful note in her voice was gone, a cold chill stealing into her gaze.

He'd known she had an ax to grind with him after the way his father had bribed her to get out of his life.

He hadn't realized how hard she'd come out swinging.

Don't miss what happens next in
Heartbreaker
by Joanne Rock, part of her Dynasties: Mesa Falls series!

Available March 2020 wherever
Harlequin Desire books and ebooks are sold.

Harlequin.com

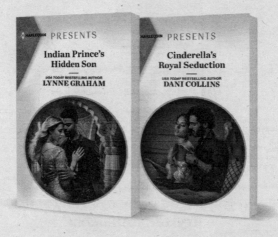

Love Harlequin romance?

DISCOVER.

Be the first to find out about promotions, news and exclusive content!

Facebook.com/HarlequinBooks

Twitter.com/HarlequinBooks

Instagram.com/HarlequinBooks

Pinterest.com/HarlequinBooks

ReaderService.com

EXPLORE.

Sign up for the Harlequin e-newsletter and download a free book from any series at **TryHarlequin.com**

CONNECT.

Join our Harlequin community to share your thoughts and connect with other romance readers! **Facebook.com/groups/HarlequinConnection**

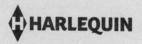

HSOCIAL2020